To Prepare or To Protect

Secrets to Solving a Parents Dilemma

By

Lori McGuire

Copyright © 2003 by Lori McGuire

To Prepare or To Protect
by Lori McGuire

Printed in the United States of America

ISBN 1-591609-27-5

All rights reserved. No part of this publication may be reproduced or transmitted in any form or by any means without written permission of the publisher.

Unless otherwise indicated, Bible quotations are taken from the King James Version/ Amplified Bible Parallel Edition. Copyright © 1995 by the Zondervan Corporation. All rights reserved.

Xulon Press
www.XulonPress.com

Xulon Press books are available in bookstores everywhere, and on the Web at www.XulonPress.com.

Table of Contents

Introduction vii

To Prepare or to Protect 15

Show them who they Are 31

Teach them to be Peaceful 49

Start small and Think Big 61

Teach them to be Thankful 75

Character and Integrity are Learned
Behaviors 89

The Pharisee Factor 123

Effective on the Battlefield 149

The Power of Choice 163

Creating a Sanctuary 183

You are Never Alone 211

Introduction

Before we get started, I want to thank you for picking up this book or borrowing it from a friend. It means a great deal to me that you're devoting your valuable time to these pages.

This is, after all, the third largest undertaking of my life.

Yes, as much as it might be better salesmanship to tell you that this is the most monumental work of my life.... well, it's not. You see, I'm married, and that's my biggest undertaking (and if you're married too, you know that it's a work in constant progress). I'm also the mother of five daughters...no, that's not a misprint; I've got FIVE of them! My children are my second tremendous – and continuous – project.

So, this book takes third place. But it is definitely a labor of love.

This book is the inspiration of my husband, my children and some truly exceptional friends. It is my belief that, once you've achieved something sensational, that you have the responsibility to share it with others. And I have indeed accomplished something of great importance. It is simply this – I LOVE MY LIFE!

I'm not just saying that. I mean that I truly LOVE my life. I wake up every morning and am glad to have other day to spend in this world.

This phenomenon doesn't occur just by happenstance. There are reasons my life is so satisfying, and this book is the best method I have for sharing them with as many people as possible.

It wasn't always this good, though. My life was pretty routine – except for the five children, that is – and I couldn't always say that I loved my life either. I'm sure you have days like this – when you look at your life and say to yourself, "This is it?"

You might find yourself feeling a little like a young boy we encountered on a family trip to Florida last year. The youngster and his parents had been on the same flight as ours. It was an early morning flight and it had been a long day. After arriving in Florida, we had a long way for the shuttle to take us to rental car lot, and this young man had fallen asleep on the shuttle bus. While he was sleeping, his parents told us how excited he was to be going to Disney World for the first time.

When the shuttle jerked to a stop, he sat up and looked out the window and, with as much anger as a child that age, can muster, he looked at the parking lot and said, "This is it?"

Maybe you're a lot like that little boy. When you were younger, you had visions of what your

To Prepare or To Protect

marriage and your family would be like. Now, though, between car pools, music lessons, braces, school plays, job stresses, laundry, bills, yard work, relatives, friends, church and social obligations, you're saying to yourself, "This is it?"

Trust me. I've been there, done that.

The fact that you picked up this book tells me something about you. Either you have children, or you're considering raising a family. This is a common bond you and I share with the rest of the world. Almost all of us have the ability to procreate. Even in cases where medical issues make it physically impossible to have a baby, we still have the ability to be parents through adoption or foster care. Because we share this common bond, we also share the anxieties, fears and triumphs that go along with it.

We also bring with us into our parenting lives events and experiences from our past, and these have a great effect on the way we raise our own children.

For instance, more people than not come from some sort of dysfunctional home situation, myself included. Whether it is something as severe as sexual abuse, or as minor as an obsessive cleaning fetish, we all bring these factors with us that contribute to the environment we create for our children.

That's not to say we are left without choices on how to handle the childhood baggage we carry with us. We may use these situations as excuses to perpetuate the same mistakes our own parents made. Or, we can take these same issues and use them as a motivation to change and do better. This is a choice that is in our hands, and it's a choice that will affect our own lives, our childrens' lives and even the lives of our grandchildren. That's because there's always a strong possibility for bad parenting decisions to be passed along from generation to generation.

I grew up in a family where one of my parents was an alcoholic. One of them was stressed and constantly full of rage. I fell in love when I was 16 with the first guy I ever dated. We got married one week after we graduated from high school and had our first child six weeks later. We had five daughters by the time we were 25.

I'm happy to say that we are still married, and there's an entire book to be written on how we've kept this marriage intact and strong. As is the case with most marriages, it hasn't always been easy.

For years, I was basically a ranting, raving lunatic. I tell people that my main mode of transportation back then was a broomstick. They think I'm kidding, and I can laugh now about it, but…oh, boy, there are some stories to tell.

The point in telling you all of this is to let you know that I have learned some basic things about children, life and happiness that have changed my life in a dramatic fashion. These are the lessons I share in the following pages.

No matter what your background is or how smart you happen to be, the most valuable tool you can have as a parent is the ability and desire to seek, sort and apply information. If you don't seek information, from any possible source, you will never find the tools that can help you be a better parent and live a better life. If you don't sort and prioritize this information,

To Prepare or To Protect

you will be overwhelmed and confused. And, if you don't apply the things you learn, you will never change and you may miss out on some of the greatest gifts life has to offer.

Important parts of this book are devoted to the need to taking an expansive view of your life and of your role as a parent. Sometimes we got so busy with the details of doing the "parenting thing" that we forget how important it is to get to know our children – I mean, really know them as people. At some point, our children are going to be adults. Then what? They are off to do their own thing, and we've spent so much time and energy trying to provide, protect and survive them that we never even get to know what kind of people they are.

All parents experience feelings of inadequacy as their children grow and change. It is scary at times to think about the enormity of our responsibilities. There is one thing I firmly believe, and it should be reassuring to all of us – there are no perfect parents. All of us are in the process of learning and growing. Even your neighbors or friends who you perceive as being picture perfect have to face their own fears, obstacles and feelings of insecurity.

Parenting, in itself, is very much like riding a bike. Someone can tell you everything you need to know about bike riding. They can explain to you how momentum and physics play key roles in your ability to stay upright. They can describe to you how it will feel when the bike veers, and how to adjust to keep from falling. Yet, when it comes right down to it, there is only one way to learn how to ride a bike.

You've got to get on and fall off a few times before you get the hang of it.

Like bike riding, parenting is an experience of constant adjustments tries and fails. And just as it is with bike riding, your success as a parent is not based on how many times you fall.

Good parents just keep getting right back up again.

Your children grow at a shockingly fast rate and are with you for a far shorter time than you could ever dream or wish. Not that my five daughters are 17, 15, 14, 11 and 10, I look at them each day and can hardly believe it. It seems that just yesterday, I was knee-deep in diapers, potty training and teething rings. Today, I am more thankful than ever that I made some critical changes in the way I view parenting, and that as a result, I haven't wasted the precious time I have with my children. I'm not claiming to be a parenting genius, but I have been open-minded and willing to learn, and I've reaped the benefits.

Everything in this book is available to anyone who is hungry for something more in their family relationships. The only key is to have an open mind and a willingness to recognize your shortcomings and a desire to change them.

The title of this book comes in the wake of disturbing events in the past few years. From the events of September 11th, to a recent untimely death of a young woman in my own community, each of us should be acutely aware that life is incredibly precious. Are we, though? It often doesn't seem so.

To Prepare or To Protect

As parents, we spend too much time and energy fighting battles that should not have to be fought. We spend too much of ourselves defending and protecting our families when we should be enjoying them.

We feel it is us against the world, and the odds are not in our favor.

In the course of this book, I'll be sharing some of my own experience. You'll see that I'm a graduate of the proverbial school of hard knocks and, hopefully, you'll be encouraged, inspired and a little bit convinced that you can shape a better, more satisfying life for yourself and your family. You will definitely evaluate your role as a parent and, just possibly, you will find room for some change in your life.

If your family is not what you dreamed it would be, if you feel like you are caught on a treadmill of anxiety, fear and frustration, don't despair. If you find yourself asking, "This is it?" maybe you'll find that there is indeed something more out there for you. You may just need to seek a little deeper, sort a little faster and apply a little harder. Life is too good to spend it frustrated, fearful and sad.

I have tried it both ways. Trust me – content, happy and peaceful is better.

CHAPTER ONE

To Prepare or Protect

Our 16-year-old daughter brought us the tragic news.

Our small, Midwestern suburb had just lost a model high school senior. She was pretty, popular, full of life and dreams and vision.

And now she was gone, lost to a car accident.

My heart ached for her parents and the pain they must be feeling. The cloud of sadness that seemed to affect everyone in our tight-knit community probably caused each parent to breathe a thankful sigh that it was not their child. I know it made me reflect on the five incredible children my husband and I are bringing up.

This was a topic of conversation among parents in our community, in our church and in the "mothers' Bible study" I attend. We wondered how we would be affected by the same situation and how others would be affected. We all know that parenting is among the most difficult things anyone is called upon to do, and we all shared an unspoken thought about raising children in today's world.

It's a dangerous world, and our children's lives are so very fragile.

And it doesn't help that parents are afflicted with so much contrary, contradicting and just plain wrong information. All of us, myself included, question the ability of our flesh to provide all that is needed to rear children in this day and age.

In the wake of school shootings, increases in teenage pregnancy, depression, abortion and teen suicide, we all should be asking ourselves, "Do we have a society-wide dilemma on our hands?" To that, I answer a definite and resounding YES!

What's both sad and infuriating, though, is that we have passed these crises off as "child problems." It never ceases to amaze me that, after each tragic incident that makes the national news or just the local paper, parents are very rarely mentioned as bearing some responsibility for what happened. I constantly wonder why parents are not held more accountable for the actions of their children – whether it is shootings in Jonesboro, Arkansas or the teenage boy and girl down the street who create a pregnancy.

After all, they are only children.

There are no shortage of documentaries about child anger, sibling rivalry, teen rebellion and increased sex and violence among high schoolers. But where are the parents in these situations?

I often wonder how many of these parents, in

To Prepare or To Protect

times of trouble, just threw up their hands and said, "What are you gonna do? Kids are just kids."

How many parents have allowed society, public opinion polls, television and the Internet to be their scapegoats in giving up on their children? If we let the television do our child raising for us, then it becomes very easy to blame TV when trouble occurs?

I wonder, along the same lines, about the much-publicized increase in attention deficit disorders and hyperactivity disorders? Please don't misunderstand me. I realize that there are legitimate diagnoses of ADD, but the increase has skyrocketed over the past ten years. While I believe that there are legitimately thousands of children who suffer from attention deficit disorder, I believe just as strongly that the only attention in which many of these kids are deficient is the attention they should be getting from their parents.

As parents, we must, at some point, take a look at cause and effect in raising children. A child's reaction to circumstances or situations is a direct effect of the influences that have been instilled in them since birth. In any given situation, a child can react in any number of ways.

Let's say, for example, a child is bullied at school. One child may just blow it off and ignore the bully's taunts. Another may seek the help of a teacher or counselor. One child may marshal the support of his friends to help defend against the bully's attacks. Yet another child will choose to take a gun to school and end his misery with a flurry of bullets.

There is cause and effect taking place here.

There is a cause for the child choosing this particular type of deadly reaction, and the effect is a number of senseless deaths.

What has happened? Have we declined as a civilization to the point that life has little, if any value?

I don't believe so. There is a little factual story I once heard that has some relevance to what's happening to families in today's world. If you put a frog in a pot of boiling water, he will jump out. However, if you put a frog in a pot of cool water and put a low flame under it, he will simmer in it until he is dead.

For the last several years, our society has been simmering.

In my grandparents' day, their biggest worries were Elvis's hips, chewing gum in school and the possibility of their adolescent male children checking out the bra section in the Sears and Roebuck catalog. Why, then, are today's parents forced to fear school shootings, mind-altering drugs, social anxiety disorders and depression? Many families are like that simmering frog, due to lack of knowledge on how to cope with this changing world. They may be simmering, but I refuse to believe that they are cooked.

There is enough information available to teach anyone how to be a better parent. The problem is not lack of information, but where to find the information that will really work.

Is it possible that, for a while now, we have gotten our thinking backwards? Maybe parents are tending to focus more on the things that we fear and dread for our children rather than devoting attention

To Prepare or To Protect

to the things they are capable of accomplishing. It seems to me that our problem is not so much seeing the threats from which we need to protect our children. Rather, we need to better understand how to focus our attentions positively and productively.

Today's information age has been a great help for parents and children in terms of doing research. It's wonderful that our kids have such a wealth of information available to them to do reports for school. On the other hand, for parents, all of this information may cause more than a few cases of "information constipation." There is such a thing as the paralysis of analysis.

I'll admit that I don't seem to have as many anxieties as many of the moms I encounter. I often wondered why that was the case, until it dawned on me – after listening to many of them discuss the dozens of new child raising theories being developed on a regular basis – that I am ambitiously lazy.

Let me explain what that means. Most parents who have tremendous anxieties about how best to raise their children are incredibly intelligent, well-read and have an intense desire to give their sons and daughters the best life possible. They read hundreds of newspaper articles, stacks of parenting magazines and scores of parenting web sites. They join groups of parents to discuss the latest trends in child-rearing. These people will go to seminars, watch talk shows devoted to parenting.... I've even known one or two to consult a psychic in their search for answers.

With all of that information – much of it conflicting – they get "information constipation."

Their minds are swimming with all of the ideas on what it takes to be a perfect parent.

And they make themselves miserable trying to cope with the shifting winds of conflicting advice. They struggle at the grocery store when their three-year-old falls to floor in a fit of rage over a candy bar. They know that one expert says discipline is a must, but another says children must be allowed to express their emotions.

A mother tells her son not to play with dolls, until her sister-in-law encourages it so that the boy can be more in touch with his sensitive side.

It's no wonder that so many parents are going to bed at night exhausted, confused and feeling like complete and utter failures.

That's where I'm fortunate to be so ambitiously lazy. I'm ambitious to be all that I can be for my family and helping them to be all that they can become. I'm lazy, though, about trying too many new techniques. I don't feel compelled to jump on the latest bandwagon on raising happy, safe and productive children.

While I'm open-minded, I'm also more than a little stubborn. When I find something that works, I stick with it and keep working at it. There is one important characteristic that, I believe, separates the confused from the confident, and that is the ability to rely on one primary, trusted source of information that we can use to measure the worthiness of all other sources.

This is true in virtually every profession. Pharmacists, nurses, pilots, accountants.... they all

To Prepare or To Protect

rely on a central, proven, dependable source of information. That's because those texts are usually written by experts who have been there, done that.

Let's face it. If you had to walk though a minefield, wouldn't you want to follow someone who had already made it through to the other side? And what is parenting, but a modern-day minefield?

I don't share many of the same anxieties as my good friends, because I also rely on just one main manual. I read a lot of books. I love to read, and I love to absorb new information, but I measure everything I read and hear according to the measuring stick given to me by my one primary source of information.

That book is the Bible.

Okay, at this point, you may be thinking that I snuck that one in on you. You're thinking that you didn't plan on buying one of "those spiritual books." Before you let your skepticism get the better of you, let me just say one thing. The purpose of this book remains the same. If you started reading because you want information on child raising and building a better life, than I would suggest you keep reading to get help on doing just that. And when you finish this book, you can sort out what you don't agree with, and apply those points with which you do agree.

Either way, I guarantee you'll get results. They may or may not be exactly the results you envisioned when you started reading, but that just depends on your sorting process.

Reading the rest of this book is going to be a lot like practicing good health care. In the medical profession, vital signs are everything. Whenever you go to the doctor, the first thing they do is check your pulse, temperature, respiratory rate and blood pressure. If you ever have surgery, your vital signs are monitored continuously to make certain you are stable.

So, in the chapters to come, we'll be discussing the areas that are the vital signs you need to monitor to measure the stability in your childrens' lives. Sometimes, people go for years without having their vital signs checked. In those cases, doctors are usually forced to undertake emergency actions to address dire situations that *may have been preventable* with an earlier checkup.

The same is true with our children. Sometimes we get so busy with our day-to-day stresses and activities that we forget to monitor our kids' vital signs. Then, when something bad happens, we have to react to a serious, but preventable, condition that occurred because we failed to keep a close watch earlier. All too often, we neglect the little events that eventually produce big difficulties. I've discovered in raising five children that, if we focus on the little things, we can avoid big problems down the road.

Thinking about this issue, there's a phrase that frequently pops into my mind. Prepare or protect? That's a question with which we're continually wrestling. How do you protect your children from the very world in which they are going to have to live? Aside from taking them to a deserted island and raising them like the Swiss Family Robinson, you realistically have very little ability to protect

To Prepare or To Protect

them from every negative influence in society.

Yet, I believe that we would not be here on this earth if there were not some way to protect ourselves from all that can and does come against us.

That was even more clear to me when I went to the Word to find for myself what God had to say about preparing or protecting. Personally, I like to study from different versions of the Bible, but that day I was studying from the King James Version. I found "prepare", "prepared", "preparedst", "prepareth", "preparing", "preparation" — all in all, I found some version of the world "prepare" used 200 times in the King James Version.

The Greek, or New Testament, definition of the root word "prepare" is particularly instructive:

> *To provide or **make ready for by internal means or external means**, to establish, a vessel or implement or equipment used to make ready for, literally such as a wife to a husband **or a mother to a child.***

It is apparent that we, as parents, are created by God to be the vessel that provides for our children everything that it takes to be stable, established, ready for life in this world, clean, holy and consecrated. Preparing is a big job. Thankfully, God has provided us with everything we need in the main manual and He is, after all, the creator of the product.

Surprisingly, the root word "protect" is used just one time in the King James Version of the Bible, in Duet. 32:38. The Hebrew translation of the word "protection" is:

To cover or shield from injury, or destruction, to defend, or guard.

Hey, don't start panicking here, wondering why the word "protect" is only found once in the Bible when you've always thought of God as your protector. Let's look at this a little deeper. I'm going to do a little paraphrasing of the lessons found in Deuteronomy 32.

In that chapter, Moses is speaking to the people of Israel. He is reminding them that God has prepared them to enter this new land. He reminds the people that God had provided everything that they needed to get to this place, and yet the people had turned away from God to do their own thing.

The people of Israel were embracing other gods and perversions of all sorts. They were impatient with God's way of doing things and felt that everything would be better in their own hands. They were about to enter into the Promised Land in which they knew there was tremendous prosperity. They had taken their eyes off of God and put them on themselves. They had become selfish, and found other, more tangible things that they could rely upon and refer to as gods.

Verse 17: *They sacrificed unto devils not to God; to gods whom they knew not, to new gods that came newly up, whom your fathers feared not. 18 of the Rock that*

> *begat thee thou are unmindful and hast forgotten God that formed thee. 19 And when the Lord saw it, he abhorred them, because of the provoking of his sons and of his daughters. 20 And he said I will hide my face from them, I will see what their end shall be: for they are a very froward generation, children in whom is no faith. 21 They have moved me to jealousy with that **which is not** God; they have provoked me to anger with their vanities; and I will move them to jealousy with those which are not a people; I will provoke them to anger with a foolish nation. (King James Version)*

It continues to express God's anger at how the people had become. It is Verse 36 that contains the important passage about "protection."

> Verse 36: *For the Lord shall judge his people and repent himself for his servants, when he seeth that **their** power is gone, and there is none shut up or left. 37 And he shall say, Where are **their** gods, **their** rock in whom they trusted, 38 which did eat the fat of their sacrifices and drank the wine of their drink offerings? Let them rise up and help you, and be your **protection.*** (King James Version)

We see through these passages that people had

the power to overcome *anything* that came against them when they chose to trust and rely on God. We can also see that God gave them an important choice – either trust or don't trust Him.

There is a strong and important correlation between that time and our present day.

We are living in one of the most prosperous times ever in the history of the world, but what have we allowed to become our gods? Where do we seek advice on what is best for our families?

There are thousands upon thousands of experts and publications telling us what is best for our children, everything we need to know from potty training to college. We need to ask ourselves, though, if we're weighing these sources against the main manual. *The sin is not in the seeking; the sin is in the* ***reliance*** *upon something other than what God said.* Is it wrong to have questions? No, of course not. It's where you go to get your answers that will get you in trouble. **You see God doesn't protect us by shielding or hiding us from the world and all its problems. Our protection is found in us being *prepared* to face those problems, and recognize them as part of life.**

Basically God is telling us, as parents, "You think you're so smart. Even though I've provided you with all the information you need to prepare your family for this world, you have decided to try other ways. You have made the media and man your gods in your time of stress and confusion and frustration. Ok, I will respect your choice and now let's see if they will help you in your time of need. When

To Prepare or To Protect

---

your child loses control and shoots his classmates, turn to your experts for help. When your teenage daughter is pregnant, go to the physiologist and find out where you went wrong."

God is a jealous God. He loves us, but he also allows us free will to choose to be obedient or not, to trust him or not, to sort out his word and rely upon it or not.

We see this lesson at work every day. Once, my daughter was hanging on the rod in her closet and swinging back and forth. As I walked in, she had flipped herself upside down and was hanging from her knees. I told her, "Please don't do that. That rod is not designed to be a monkey bar. It's going to break, and you'll get hurt."

She answered back, "No, it won't. I do this all the time, and *all my friends* do this in their closets too." Just then, the bar snapped and Bridget landed on her head. A second later, for emphasis, the bar came down and smacked her across the back.

As she let out a wail, I told her, "This is a prime example of what disobedience will get you. I tried to tell you what would happen, but you thought you knew better than I did. ***So you got exactly what I tried to spare you from getting.***"

One can only wonder, what unhappy events could God spare our families from experiencing if we believed that He knew more about our needs than we do?

In the earlier verses in this chapter, there is a statement that needs to be revisited because of its tremendous impact. It is in verse 20:

*And he said I will hide my face from them, I will see what their end shall be: for they are a very **froward** generation, children in whom there is no faith.*

The word "froward" in this text means to turn away from, to be contrary, to become perverse, to change or become converted, or *to get off course.* How many of us have turned away from or gotten off course of what God has intended for our family lives? How many of us have been swayed by certain activists that promote lifestyles that contradict God's word?

I'm not simply talking about controversial areas like homosexuality, divorce and teenage sexuality. Beyond those, think about the other gods in your life that cause conflict with what God has to say about the responsibilities of being a parent. After all, God says "sin is sin" and "it is the *little* foxes that spoil the vine." We need to look at our everyday activities.

Think about how much time you spend on entertainment and social activities that *don't* include your children. Think about how and when you discipline your children. Is your work schedule out of balance? How much time do you spend on the phone? Do you judge, criticize, condemn or complain about or around your children? Are **you** taking responsibility for bringing up your children the right way, or are you relying on other sources to do it?

There are parents who believe that the Sunday school teacher is responsible for teaching their children about living a Christian life. No, they won't

To Prepare or To Protect

admit it, but it's obvious in their approach to child rearing. Putting your children in Sunday school class once a week no more makes them a Christian, than putting them in the garage once a week would make them a car!

All of us who are parents need to understand that it is not our "job" to protect our children. That is God's job. He tells us in his Word that **He** is to be our shelter in times of trouble, and our shield in times of need. **God's job is to protect. Our job is to believe that he will.**

If we don't believe that God will protect us, and do a much better job of it than we can do ourselves, then we become like those referred to in Verse 20 – children without faith, from whom He will hide Himself. Can you imagine living your life with God hiding His face from you?

That's why I feel such a strong responsibility in my heart to share my thoughts and experiences with you. I have been set free from most of the fears and anxieties that keep so many parents in bondage, and it is indeed the truth that set me free and can do the same for you.

Stop relying on the worldly gods. You may have become "froward" and not even realized it. But if you can turn *away from*, that only means that you can still turn *back to* God. God always takes us back. He realizes that we sometimes get off track and don't even realize it.

When you are feeling overwhelmed and out of control, it's time to check the vital signs. Go back to the main manual and find out where you got off track, and then get back on.

Protecting your children is not a matter of wearing bike helmets, seatbelts and stocking caps in the cold winter. That's just common sense. The tougher, and more important, job concerns those things over which you don't have control. How can we possibly think that we can protect our children from things of the world? We have to live in the world, but thank God we are not of it.

There is only one way to assure yourself that your children will not become victims of the world, and that is to PREPARE them for it.

CHAPTER TWO

Show Them Who They Are

In writing this book, I definitely don't want to create the impression that I view my family as a perfect, pristine model of what family life should be.

Hey, we have our moments of temporary insanity just like you do. Fortunately, they are fewer and farther between all the time. We are a work in progress, just like everyone else.

The key to remember is that none of us are perfect parents. We are all growing and learning and developing skills. It's a never-ending process. As we continue on this path, we'll make mistakes. We know, though, that God promises he will never leave us or forsake us. Just knowing that will make the effort, the trials and the occasional missteps easier to deal with.

Now, let's talk about some of those vital signs I

mentioned earlier.

It is vital that our children know who they are, and exactly how special they are. This is critical if they are to grow up to be confident, forward-looking individuals.

As parents, of course we tell our children all of the time that they are special. Have you ever noticed, though, that young children in particular always want to see proof of any claim you make? Well, we can give them the proof that they are special, because it is found in the Word.

This kind of proof can have a tremendous impact on a small child. Do you ever wonder why a child finds it so easy to believe in God? You tell small children that Jesus loves them and they believe it and embrace it as fact. This gets a little more difficult as your sons and daughters get older and encounter others who may not be quite as encouraging where God's Word is concerned. That just makes it all the more important to establish the principle early that your children are different, are special, are valued and loved.

By the way, if you already have older children and think it's too late to establish these principles, just remember that the Word does not respect the whims of time. There may be more barriers to overcome in working with teenagers and even pre-teens, but it's far from impossible.

The best way to prove to your children that God has a special plan for them is to know that He has one for you too. Let's look at a few scriptures that will help encourage you to realize how special *you* are. After all, you may need it as much as your children. You cannot pass on what you don't possess yourself.

> Jeremiah 1:5: *Before I formed you in the womb **I knew and approved of you** (as my chosen instrument), and before you were born I separated and set you apart, consecrating you; (and) I appointed you as a prophet unto the nations. (Amplified)*

Just in case you think God was addressing Himself only to Jeremiah, let's clear that misconception up immediately. Aren't we all called to share the gospel, making us all prophets to the nations? And, we already know that "God is no respecter of persons," as is told to us in Acts 10:34, so we know, that just as He knew and approved of Jeremiah, He also knows and approves of us. He told Isaiah the same thing in Isaiah 49:1.

Just in case you need a little more persuasion, let's check out Romans 8:29:

> *For those whom He foreknew (of whom He was aware and **loved beforehand** He also destined from the beginning (foreordaining them) to be molded into the image of His Son (and share inwardly His likeness) that He might become the firstborn among many brethren. (Amplified)*

The amazing thing about God is that He loves

and knows everyone, even if they don't always believe it. Once you choose to believe it, though, it's amazing how the knowledge of God's love can work wonders in your life.

It's not easy, even with the security of this knowledge, to raise your children in a Christian environment. It is the nature of young people to want to "fit in" with their peers. It's not easy for them to take a stand against peer pressure unless you successfully instill in them the idea that being different is a good thing.

How often do parents hear the phrase "everyone does it" from their children, as in "Mom, everyone else is going…" or "Dad, everyone is buying it…"? One thing my children learned very early in life is that the phrase "everyone else does" just won't cut it. They can say it, but it will never be an acceptable reason for doing anything.

When my girls play the "everyone else is going" card with me, my response is always the same. I tell them that they are not like everyone else. They are special. They are set apart. They have purpose.

Often, they respond to me by saying "everyone thinks I'm weird."

To that, I tell them…you are not weird, you are peculiar.

Maybe I'd better explain that one a little bit.

Let me quote some scripture to put that word "peculiar" in proper context.

> Ex 19:5 *Now therefore if you will obey My voice in truth and keep My covenant,*

*then you shall be My own **peculiar** possession and treasure from among and above all peoples for all the earth is Mine. (Amplified)*

Deut 14:2 *For you are a holy people (set apart) to the Lord your God and the Lord has chosen you to be a **peculiar** people to himself, above all the nations on the earth. (Amplified)*

Deut 26:18 *And the Lord has declared this day that you are His **peculiar** people as He promised you, and you are to keep all His commandments. (Amplified)*

Titus 2:14 *Who gave Himself on our behalf that He might redeem us (purchase our freedom) from all iniquity and purify for Himself a people (to be **peculiar** His own, people who are) eager and enthusiastic about (living a life that is good and filled with) beneficial deeds. (Amplified)*

I Peter 2:9 *But ye are a chosen generation, a royal priesthood, a holy nation, a **peculiar** people. That ye should show forth the praises of Him who hath called you out of darkness into His marvelous light. (KJV)*

You see, peculiar has a wonderful meaning when translated from Greek or Hebrew. In Hebrew, it means *a special shut up treasure or jewel saved for special occasions*. In Greek, it simply means, *beyond special*.

What child wouldn't want to be considered "beyond special?" Given the choice to be "just like everyone else" or "beyond special", which would you choose?

We have to demonstrate this point, though, in *our* daily lives, and we can best do that by protecting ourselves from those actions that "everyone else" does, even at the adult level. This extends to the kinds of television shows we watch, to the movies we see, to the way we spend our time. This state of peculiarity that God has for us comes with the understanding that we *believe* we are special enough to live *our* lives in ways that has nothing to do with what "everyone else" is doing with theirs.

Examine your own life. Maybe you could trim or change some things that are keeping you from fulfilling *your* call to be truly peculiar. Once you've done that, share with your children the changes you've made in your own life, when appropriate. Tell them that you understand how hard it is to be different, but that it's worth it. Tell them you're sorry that you may have expected more from them than you did from yourself.

Some friends of ours once invited us out to the movies with them. When I asked my husband what movie they wanted to see, he told me it was one that carried an R rating. Well, my kids hear pretty much everything that goes on in the house, and they know that I have told them that we do not see

To Prepare or To Protect

R-rated movies.

My husband and I discussed the matter and decided that we would suggest a different movie and, if our friends wanted to stick with their original idea, then we would just pass.

My daughter Michelle asked me, "won't you be embarrassed to tell them that you don't want to go?" This gave me a golden opportunity to tell her how important it is to me to be careful about what I see and hear because it is important to God. It is more important to me, I told her, to please God than to please other people.

Never forget. Your children are watching *and* listening to you. We need to establish to them that *we* are special so that they can see that value in themselves and understand that God cares about everything they do, desire and dream.

When they see you live out *your* peculiarity, they will want to live out their own!

Jeremiah 29: 11-13 tells us:

> *For I know that thoughts and plans that I have for you, says the Lord, thought and plans for welfare and peace and not for evil, to give you hope in your final outcome. Then when you call upon Me, and you will come and pray to Me, and I will hear and heed you. Then you will seek Me, and you will come and pray to Me, and I will hear and heed you. Then you will seek Me inquire for and require me (as vital necessity) and find Me when you search for Me*

with all your heart. (Amplified)

Psalm 40:5 *Many O Lord my God are They wonderful works which Thou hast done, and Thy thoughts which are to us-ward they can not be reckoned up in order unto Thee: if I would declare and speak of them they are more than can be numbered. (KJV)*

Psalm 139:17*How precious and weighty also are Your thoughts to me, O God! How vast is the sum of them.*

I Peter 1:4 *Whereby are given unto us exceeding great and precious promises; that by these ye might be partakers of the divine nature having escaped the corruption that is in the world. (KJV)*

Things in your child's life aren't always going to go according to plan. That's all the more reason they need to know these scriptures so that they can know, even when they've suffered setbacks, that God has great plans for them. Although we don't always see how He works, knowing that He only has good thoughts for us gives our children – and ourselves – enormous comfort.

How *you*, as an adult, respond to disappointment will prove to your children that you believe God has good thoughts and plans for you. If you despair every time things go astray, they will have doubts

To Prepare or To Protect

that you believe the same principles you're asking them to embrace.

A while back, my husband was changing career paths, moving from one company to another. The new position was much closer to home with a higher salary and more opportunity for advancement. We both felt good about the change and decided to make the leap. This came at a critical time, when we had just started to build our first new home.

The new job met expectations, and then some. He loved the staff and everything about the company and his position. We were able to add some extras to the house plan because of the increase in salary.

Then the rug was pulled out from under us.

The company announced that they were selling the division in which my husband worked, and that the company buying it would be taking it out of state. When Mike came home to give us the news, I said, "Well, we believed that this job was a blessing, so God must have something even better in mind."

Actually, I was just saying that so that *he* would feel better. But, as soon as the words left my mouth, I believed them myself. Our faith in God was well-placed. The company told everyone that they would have six months to find other employment. Mike got an offer just as the six-month period was coming to a close. Because he stayed and worked faithfully for the departing company, they gave him a large bonus before he left. His new position gave him a 40 percent increase in salary.

Hold on, the story doesn't end there. One year later, this new place of employment announced that it, too, would be sold. At that time, we had a trip to Florida planned with the kids. Mike's employers told him that they needed him to stick around because of the changes taking place, and that our vacation just couldn't happen.

When we told the girls, they didn't say a word, but we couldn't help noticing a few quiet tears appearing on their cheeks. Finally, our then 14-year-old Chelsie smiled at me and said, "God must **really** have something good planned for us this time."

In tough times, it's not enough to simply sing, "Jesus loves me, this I know for the Bible tells me so." We have to *show* our children – not just through our words, but also through our actions – that we believe Jesus loves us, and that God has good plans for us. You can take your children to church at every opportunity, but if you still fall into pieces every time life puts a little pressure on you, the example you set is going to undermine their spiritual walk.

They must hear **and** see your faith working in order for them to bring that same faith into their own lives.

It is vitally important to show your children that God does love them. It is just as important that you live your life in a way that shows you know that He loves you. If you find that you feel as if you have to work to earn God's love, you're teaching your children the same mindset. They will grow up always wondering if they have done enough to earn God's love.

Do your children know that God loves them as much as He ever will? Do they know that there is nothing they can do to make God love them more than He already does? Do you know this?

Just before Jesus' physical body died on the cross, he stated, "It is finished." Many people think he was talking about his life, but what Jesus had actually finished was His very purpose for coming to earth. He accomplished what He was sent to do. Everything that Jesus gave you through his death was given to you at that moment. Even though we do sin, and even though we fall short, that does not change the fact that God loves us.

> Romans 8:38-39 *For I am persuaded beyond doubt (am sure) that neither death nor life nor angels nor principalities, nor things impending and threatening nor things to come, nor powers, 39 Nor height nor* **depth nor anything else in all creation will be able to separate us from the love of God which is in Christ Jesus our Lord.** *(Amplified)*

Sometimes we make the mistake of confusing rewards with love. Now, we are definitely rewarded in this life for obedience to the Word. But, in those times when we have perhaps put God on our back burner, we don't feel like we are blessed. The fact of the matter is that blessings are the result of living an obedient life.

Don't confuse this, though, with love. God loves the disobedient just as much as he does the obedient. We have to be careful to show our children that no matter what, God loves them.

In fact, God loves us so much He gave us the right to be disobedient.

I like my children to keep their rooms clean. I'm not a taskmaster in this respect. I don't ask for perfection. My request is that the dirty clothes be put in the hamper and the shoes in the closet. I also like for the beds to be made everyday. I provide my children with a good example by keeping my room clean and my bed made. On occasion (more often than I like) my girls do not obey.

They make excuses like "I'm too busy to make my bed" or "I like it when my clothes are on the floor." When I notice that one of the girls has been diligent about making her bed and keeping her room neat, I might give that child something special for a treat or we may make a special excursion for ice cream. Now, does that mean I love my other, slightly messier, children less? Absolutely not! We, as parents, get unhappy when our children are disobedient, but we don't love them any less.

God is even more capable of this unconditional love, because His very makeup is love.

We can do a great deal of damage to our children if *our* behavior indicates we are constantly trying to earn love from God that He has already freely given. If you are trying endlessly to get something you already have, you will be one very frustrated person. If you insist on trying to earn God's love, your children will inevitably equate your frustration and desperation with the relationship you have with God.

Think about the love you have for your own children. How much would it break your heart if one of your children thought you didn't love them, if they thought they had not sufficiently "earned" your love? How much desperation would you feel if there was no convincing this child that your love was as strong and unconditional as humanly possible? How tormented would you feel?

Yet, that is what many of us do to God. I've been there. For years, I felt that I had to work my way into God's favor. The most important revelation we can understand is that God's love is free. There is not one single thing we can do to make Him love us more. This is the very foundation on which a process of spiritual maturation can take place.

Again, you cannot teach your children something that you do not believe yourself.

> Hosea 14:4 *I will heal their faithlessness;* ***I will love them freely,*** *for my anger is turned away from them. (Amplified)*
>
> Psalms 107:43 *Who so is wise, and will observe these things even they shall understand the loving kindness of the Lord. (KJV)*
>
> Isa 54:14 *For the mountain shall depart and the hills be removed but My kindness shall not depart from thee. (KJV)*
>
> John 3:16 *For God so loved the world that he gave his only Son, so that who ever*

> *believes, relies and trusts in Him shall not die but have everlasting life. (Amplified)*

Jesus said, "freely you have received, freely give." You have to *receive* the love of God freely and then you can freely give it to your children.

In addition to knowing that your children are loved and cared for, it is important that they know and understand that the world does not have much to offer that is worth having compared to what God can help them attain. It is vitally important that they know they are *powerful* when they are hooked up with God.

> Luke 10:19 *Behold I give unto you **power** to tread on serpents and scorpions, and over all the power of the enemy: and nothing shall by any means hurt you. (KJV)*

> I Cor 4:20 *For the Kingdom of God consists of and is based on not talk but **power** (moral power and excellence of soul). (Amplified)*

> Eph 3:20 *Now unto him that is able to do exceeding abundantly above all that we ask or think, **according to the power that worketh in us.** (KJV)*

> 2 Tim 1:7 *For God did not give us a spirit of timidity (cowardice, of craven and cringing and fawning fear) but (**He has**

To Prepare or To Protect

given us a spirit) of power and of love and of a calm and well-balanced mind and discipline and self-control. (Amplified)

According to the Word, we are more than conquerors, always triumphant and always victorious. That is definitely power! I would suggest that you read these scriptures to your children and then see their reactions. I can't tell you how many times I have quoted 2 Tim 1:7 to my children when they say they are afraid to try something.

The greatest fear that most young people express to me is the fear of looking stupid or inferior to their peers. One day my daughter told me that she was intimidated by a group of older students at school. She and this older group had mutual friends, so they crossed paths frequently.

When I asked her why she felt intimidated, she told me, "I'm not afraid *of them*, but I'm afraid that I will say or do something that will make me look stupid in front of them."

It felt wonderful to tell her, "You have nothing to worry about. You have an incredible way with people. Everywhere you have ever gone, people like you. Besides that, you have not been given a spirit of fear." Occasionally, my children get annoyed with me when I preach to them. They listen, though, when their father and I encourage them to realize the power they have within them.

When it comes to facing and overcoming fears, my children have truly excelled and that is such a fulfilling and rewarding realization for a parent. I can only give the glory to God because they (after much repetition) do believe that they indeed possess the power to overcome.

Once, Chelsie was out shooting free throws in the yard and was feeling progressively discouraged with each missed shot. She said, "I can't shoot free throws. I am so bad at this." Her older sister Colleen was rebounding for her and said, "You can do this. You have in you everything you need. You can do all things." Moments like those are what we live for as parents. When your children believe they have power in a balanced way, they can face any challenge from which you may think you have to protect them.

This belief in their ability to overcome is the best possible defense mechanism against discouragement, self-doubt, embarrassment, peer pressure and anything else that can attack their self-esteem.

The best way to convince your children that the Word is true is to study the power that has been given to you and to walk in it. Face your fears and don't be shy about telling how great it feels to overcome them.

I used to have the same fear of people that my children have expressed to me. In my case, I tried to hide it behind obnoxious behavior, but that wasn't an answer. Once I realized that the power was in me to overcome the obstacle of fear, I felt I could face anything. God promises us that we are powerful; it is our job to believe Him and then walk in that power. If you won't do it for yourself, do it for your children.

Don't just tell your children about God. Show them exactly how good He is. It is critical that parents step forward and dare to believe God.

I've known so many adults who have poor self-images, and I realize that if someone had just taken the time to show them who they were when they were young, they would most likely be totally different people living totally different lives. In God's eyes, our children are special, well cared for, loved and powerful. *Showing* your children who they are in Christ – and not just telling them – is the very first step to preparing them for the world, a world they are *in* but not *of.*

CHAPTER THREE

Teach them to be Peaceful

∞

We live in a society in which stress and anxiety disorders are at an all-time high. We have road rage, child abuse, an epidemic of depression and a panorama of personality disorders. It is, to say the least, a difficult world.

It could be a lot less difficult if more people understood the power of peace. And it will definitely be a better world if we teach peacefulness to our children.

Scripture teaches us that peace is powerful. It's worth seeking and striving for. In fact, scripture gives us a sense of urgency to strive for peace in our own lives.

> I Peter 3:10-11: *For let him who wants to enjoy life and see good days (good whether apparent or not) keep his tongue free from evil and his lips from guile*

*(treachery and deceit) 11 Let him turn away from wickedness and shun it, and let him do right. Let him search for peace (harmony; undisturbedness from fears, agitating passions, and moral conflicts) and seek it eagerly (**Do not merely desire peaceful relations with God, with your fellowmen and with yourself, but pursue, go after them**) (Amplified)*

James 3:18 *And the harvest of righteousness (of conformity to God's will in thought and deed) is (the fruit of the seed) sown in peace by those who **work for and make peace** (in themselves and in others, that peace which means concord, agreement, and harmony between individuals, with undisturbedness, In peaceful mind free from fears and agitating passions and moral conflicts.) (Amplified)*

When Jesus knew that his death and ascension into heaven were near, he did something very interesting. He *left* his peace with the people closest to Him. He sent the Holy Spirit later, but He left his peace. That tells us the importance Jesus placed on peace. Take a look at John 14:27.

Peace I leave with you; My (own) peace I now give and bequeath to you. Not as the world gives do I give to you. Do not let your hearts be troubled, neither let them *be afraid. **(Stop allowing yourselves to be agitated and disturbed; and do not permit yourselves to be fearful and intimidated and cowardly and unsettled.)** (Amplified)*

"I give *and* bequeath" is the wording in the Amplified Bible. Jesus did not simply give peace to us. His peace is not like a sweater you get for Christmas and never wear. The word bequeath means "to give or leave as a personality trait, to transfer or commit." Jesus didn't just offer us peace as a tool that we might need one day when we're in a fix. He gave us *His* personality trait.

And He didn't stop there. He also gives us the command that we not *let* our hearts be troubled or afraid. He gave us the understanding that we do possess the ability to be peaceful, and that we have the free will to put that ability to work.

Perhaps the people who can best understand the importance of peace are those who had the hardest time finding it. I place myself in that category. I was probably the most UN-peaceful person you could ever meet. On the surface, I could act serene as a placid lake on a still day. Inside, though, I was tormented with rage, fears and anxieties about everything, issues big and small.

Today, I tell my children to seek peace. Matthew 6:33 states, "Seek ye first the kingdom and then all these things will be added unto you." If you and your children will seek peace, you will be able to overcome those matters that would steal your peace from you. Nothing will make the devil flee faster than refusing to give up your inner peace. Because we have a houseful of females, you can imagine how invaluable peace is to my poor husband. Between raging hormones and the everyday pains of adolescence, we would all be nuts by now if we weren't constantly striving for peace.

I always tell my girls (when they push me to the limits of my patience), "I am not going to lose my peace over this."

My lessons on peace would have no impact on my daughters, however, if I hadn't been able to find peace myself.

There was a turning point for peace for our family, and it was a moment that proved God is real and that walking in peace allows you to experience something that truly passes all understanding. Things that wouldn't affect the average person would send me into fits of rage. I would yell, scream, stop, and even throw things. My family had entire days ruined because of my tantrums. No doubt, my children spent countless hours in their rooms, hiding from me so they wouldn't be the objects of my wrath.

One thing that always ignited my fuse was to be late. I don't like to be late for anything. Yet, for some reason, (now I believe it was God's way of trying to sand off my rough edges), my family was habitually late for everything. Getting to church on Sunday morning was always a major battle. I would get up an extra hour early in order to make breakfast, clean the dishes (coming back home to a dirty kitchen would also set off my uncontrollable rage),

To Prepare or To Protect

and get all of my little princesses dressed. My best laid plans, though, rarely worked. Someone would have a hole in her tights. A shoe would be missing. And Mike would never get up until the last minute.

Invariably, my heart would start pounding and I would begin yelling, "It never fails," I would scream, "I work and work and work to get us off to church on time and one of you always messes things up. Nobody cares about mommy."

The irony of this escaped me. Here I was, ranting and raving so that my family could go to church and meet this God that mommy said she loves so much. And while I was throwing a fit, I was insisting that my children walk in peace. No fussing, no fighting, no complaining and absolutely no whining.

One morning, we were getting ready to go to school. Mike had already left for work, and the girls and I were still at home. As usual, we were running late. I was rushing around trying to find a missing backpack. Then, Molly – our youngest – who was six at the time suddenly remembered she needed to bring a snack. I could feel that familiar heart pounding feeling beginning and felt the scream begin to well up in my throat, but this time I decided to fight against my urge to explode.

I instructed Molly to go to the pantry and fill a small bag with pretzels while I kept looking for her backpack. She pulled out a huge five-pound bag of pretzels, holding it from the bottom instead of the top. Naturally, waves of pretzels went crashing to the floor.

At that moment, time seemed to stop. Molly's

sisters scattered knowing the verbal explosion was about to begin. Molly stood there clutching the empty bag of pretzels, the knuckles of her little fingers turning white. I watched as the ocean of pretzels made its way under the refrigerator. The two enormous tears filled Molly's eyes that in the past fueled my rage somehow this time softened my heart. I looked at the pretzels one more time, then at Molly, and I felt a huge smile begin to broaden on my face. "WHOA," I said, "that is a LOT of pretzels." I waded across the sea of pretzels, gave Molly a big hug and said, "Don't worry about it. I'll clean it up when I get home."

My heart stopped pounding, and I felt absolutely great. I had done it. I had *chosen*, strived for and found peace.

We got in the van for the drive to school. All the girls were sitting in silence. Molly plopped herself into her seat and buckled in. Her sisters waited in trepidation at the angry lecture that was still sure to come. Molly smiled and said, "Mom didn't even get mad at me." Bridget exclaimed, "NO WAY!" The course of the entire day, theirs and mine, was completely changed by me *choosing* peace instead of *reacting* in rage.

That day my children *knew* there was a GOD.

That was the beginning of a wonderful road to peace, and I very rarely lose control anymore.

There are some incredible scripture verses that can encourage and maybe even convince us to see that the level of peace we pursue will affect our relationship with God.

2 Corinthians 13:11 *Finally brethren, farewell, be perfect, be of good comfort, be of one mind, live in peace; and the God of love and peace shall be with you. (KJV)*

Eph 2:12-14 *(Remember) that you were at that time separated (living apart) from Christ (excluded from all part in Him, utterly estranged and outlawed from the rights of Israel as a nation, and strangers with no share in the sacred compacts of the promise, with no knowledge of or right in God's agreements, His covenants) And you had no home (no promise); you were in the world without God. 13 But now in Christ Jesus you who were once (so) far away, through the blood of Christ have been brought near. 14 For **He is our peace (our bond of unity and harmony)** He has made us both one (body) and has broken down (destroyed abolished) the hostile dividing wall between us. (Amplified)*

Hebrews 12:14 *Strive to live in peace with everybody and pursue that consecration and holiness without which no one will (ever) see the Lord. (Amplified)*

Isaiah 54:13 *And all thy children shall be taught of the Lord; and **great** shall be the peace of thy children. (KJV)*

These verses tell us that walking in peace is not a passive event. It takes action on our part. In the first scripture, we see that we must take action and live in peace. In the second, we see that we must *believe* that there is a peace that was provided for us, through the shed blood of Christ. Finally, we see that we have an obligation to live in peace because this verse in Hebrews refers to our duty as Christians to walk in peace so that others will see the nature of God in us through our behavior.

Living, believing and fulfilling this obligation brings us into a close relationship with God because God blesses obedience.

Scripture also tells us that peace can help us overcome adversity.

> I Corinthian 14:33 *For God is not the author of confusion, but of peace, as in all the churches of the saints. (KJV)*

> Colossians 3:15 *And let the peace (soul harmony with comes) from Christ rule (act as the umpire continually) in your hearts (deciding and settling with finality all questions that arise in your minds, in that peaceful state) to which as (members of Christ's) one body you were also called to live. And be ye thankful (appreciative), (giving thanks to God always). (Amplified)*

> Philippians 4:7 *And God's peace (shall be yours, that tranquil state of soul assured of*

> *its salvation through Christ and so fearing nothing from God and being content with its earthly lot of whatever sort that is, that peace) which **transcends all understanding** shall garrison and mount guard over your hearts and minds in Christ Jesus. (Amplified)*
>
> John 16:33 *I have told you these things so that in Me you may have (perfect) peace and confidence. In the world you will have tribulation and trials, and distress, and frustration; but be of good cheer (take courage, be confident, certain and undaunted) for I have overcome the world. (I have deprived it of power to harm you and have conquered it for you) (Amplified)*

In these scriptures, we see that the peace to which we have access allows us to overcome a gamut of challenges that most of us encounter every day. We see that peace will allow us to make confident, stable decisions.

Also, peace helps increase our access to knowledge and wisdom.

> James 3:17 *But the wisdom that is from above is first pure, **then peaceful, and gentle and easy to be entreated**, full of mercy and good fruits, without partiality and without hypocrisy. (KJV)*

> Proverbs 3:17 *Her (wisdom) ways are highways of pleasantness and all her paths are peace. (Amplified)*
>
> 2 Timothy 1:2 *May grace (God's favor) and peace (which is perfect well being, all necessary good, all spiritual prosperity and freedom from fears and agitating passions and moral conflicts) be multiplied to you in (full, personal, precise and correct) knowledge of God and of Jesus our Lord. (Amplified)*

It's easy to see why Jesus has put such a high priority on peace. Peace affects our personal relationship with God, our power to overcome emotional instability, and the level of knowledge and wisdom in which we walk.

The very first step to establishing peace in your children is to make peace a priority in your own life. Your children will mimic what you do, especially when they are very young. If a dropped egg on the floor will throw you into a tantrum – as it did with me – then you have not made peace a priority. There is no magic prayer that will establish peace within us. It takes discipline and effort, but it will be well worth it.

Striving for peace myself has had reverberations throughout our entire family. One day, Michelle, my ten-year-old, lost her schoolbooks and feared missing her bus. I heard her begin to cry, and then she stopped, took a deep breath and said, "I am not

To Prepare or To Protect

going to lose my peace over this." It made me feel grateful that I had discovered the importance of peace and, in so doing, had helped my child learn to grasp that very same principle.

Our daughter Chelsie has a perfectionist-type personality. With that personality type comes a great deal of frustration, worry and anxiety because life, by its nature, does not lend itself to perfection. Chelsie loves schedules, agendas and plans. Unfortunately, in a large household such as ours, chaos has the upper hand over organization and planning. This has been a long struggle for her, and I am constantly telling her that nothing is so important that it is worth losing your peace. If you give up your peace, I tell her, you have lost something very important **and** you haven't changed your situation either.

Chelsie plays tennis. When I got to her match one day just before she was about to start, I said to her through the fence, "How's it going?" She looked at me with a pained but determined expression and said, "Well, I think I left my algebra books on the picnic table outside the school (which was a mile away), but I'm not going to lose my peace."

Normally, I would have been elated to hear Chelsie say that, but past experience had taught me to expect an emotional explosion any minute. Much to my surprise, she contained herself during her match. Each time she and her opponent would change sides, she would look at me through the fence and say, "I'm keeping my peace, no matter how hard it is."

This encouraged me, but then she was down two

sets to her opponent. I was certain the tears would flow, panic would set it and it would be all over but the crying. She came to fence for a drink, looked at me, smiled and said, "I've lost my books, I'm losing my match, but I AM NOT GOING TO LOSE MY PEACE!" She came back and won the match. I went to the school and her books were still there, and I could not have been more thankful.

If you have a child with an extreme perfectionist personality, you can certainly understand my joy. That day was a huge turning point for Chelsie. In the car on the way home, she said, "I'm glad that I didn't lose it out there. On the inside, I wanted to fall apart, but I just kept telling myself that *everything is going to work out*."

If your children see you start to strive for peace, they will know there is a God and that His word works. My older girls have been able to witness this firsthand in me. I was such a raving lunatic, but because I have tried to make peace a priority, I've been able to show my daughters how God works in all of us.

We have found that the Word does work. All you have to do is take a step of faith, and God will meet you right where you are. Make peace a priority in your life. Your light will shine to your children and they will want what you have. If you stay peaceful, they will see the love of God reflected through you. Jesus said, "Blessed are the peacemakers." Be blessed, and through you, your children will be blessed.

CHAPTER FOUR

Start Small and Think Big

∽

As I've thought about my life over the past few years and how much it has changed, I can't help but think about how much my perception of God has changed as well.

One of the biggest mistakes I believe we can make as parents is not investing time in our own relationship with God. We spend countless hours teaching our children. We may even spend a great deal of time in church, in bible studies, in church-related activities, but do we spend enough time develop our own personal, intimate relationship with God? At times, I've felt guilty about not even coming close to the kind of Christian I wanted to be. Sometimes, we feel so frustrated about our inability to achieve that desired relationship with God that we settle for some religious routine that makes us feel as if we're doing "ok."

When we settle for less, though, we are actually walking away from the best experiences we – and our families – could ever achieve.

The fact is that God is big, but building a relationship with him starts small.

When I was growing up, I would spend a lot of time just talking to God about everyday things. I would have conversations about everything going on in my life, about what was making me happy or sad, about how I knew He was always there even though I couldn't see Him. All of these conversations had to be very private, because no one I knew thought you could talk to God like that. The image of God we were taught was completely different than the God I knew.

When I got older and found a group of friends who were Christians, I noticed that they also believed in talking to God, but the topic of conversation was different. The group with which I was involved were wonderful people who loved God, but the main focus of this group was prosperity.

I had never heard any kind of prosperity message in the church within which I had grown up. In fact, I had always heard much the contrary. This new message was appealing though. I had the door open to a whole new concept of God. While these prosperity messages concerned a great deal of truth, they in themselves can become a dangerous form of religious bondage. Nothing in God's word is bad or dangerous, but what we do with God's word can cause our lives to get out of balance and out of focus.

To Prepare or To Protect

Over the next few years, I went from one form of religious bondage to another. The first taught me that I was nothing, and completely unable to ever know God or relate to Him. The other taught me that I was everything – and entitled to everything. Both approaches carried hazards. In both cases, I followed all the rules to the best of my ability. In the first, I never felt any kind of closeness to God. In the second, not only did I not feel close to God, but I also didn't prosper the way I was being taught I should.

Basically, I saw myself as a complete spiritual failure.

If you see yourself in these words, take the time to ask yourself two questions:

- Am I growing in my relationship with God in a steady, consistent way?

- Is my life *progressively* improving in *every* area – spiritually, in relationships, family, finances, righteousness, peace and joy?

If your answers to these questions are "no", the good news is that the course of your life can be changed. No matter what your situation or your spiritual level, God has a plan for you and it is a plan of order and balance. By understanding this, you will not only live the life God has intended for you, but you will also launch your children's spiritual walk by setting a good example of how to grow spiritually every day of your life.

The book of John contains important revelations

that can completely change your attitude about developing a relationship with Jesus. In the first chapter, the Bible tells us "the word was made flesh." In other words, God's word and everything it encompasses came to earth in the form of man. Later in the same chapter, John the Baptist recognizes that Jesus *is* the Messiah. Check the wording in John 1:35-39:

> *Again the next day John was standing with two of his disciples and he looked at Jesus as He walked along, and said, "Look! There is the Lamb of God!" The two disciples heard him say this and they followed Him. But Jesus turned and as He saw them coming He said, "What are you looking for? (And what is it that you wish?) (Amplified)*

The depth of this question – what are you looking for? – is stunning. These people had the revelation that this was God's son. It's a question we all need to answer. When we first discovered Jesus, when we were first introduced to him — what were we looking for?

I guess the answer depends a great deal on how we were introduced.

You see up to this point, God had been delivering his people out of their messes for thousands of years. Over and over, he would deliver them, and yet I don't believe it was ever God's intention to be seen as our fairy godfather. Sometimes, without meaning

To Prepare or To Protect

to, this is what we teach our children.

When we came to Jesus, were we looking for a lifelong friend and commitment, or were we looking for a miracle? If you realize the depth of your relationship with God, you received both. You received the miracle of salvation, and you received a lifelong friend.

The question is…. *what were you looking for?*

Let's look at again at the book of John. In John 2:1-4, Jesus had *just* met and chosen his disciples.

> *And on the third day there was a marriage in Cana of Galilee; and the mother of Jesus was there: And both Jesus was called and his disciples to the marriage. And when they wanted wine the Mother of Jesus said to him, "They have no wine." Jesus saith unto her, "Woman what have I to do with this, my hour is not yet come?" (KJV)*

As I studied this, I could almost sense what Jesus must have been feeling. He had just met and chosen his disciples. I would venture to think that he wanted them to get to know him as a person and a friend before he began performing miracles. I believe that Jesus wanted them to trust his *message* – more than his miracle-working ability. When we miss the message and seek the miracle, we miss what Jesus came to do for us. I believe he wants us to seek his face and not just his hand, to understand that we don't have to live relying on miracles to carry us from crisis to crisis.

> Ephesians 2:12-13 *That at the time you were without Christ, being aliens from the common wealth of Israel and strangers from the covenants of promise, having no hope, and without God in the world. But now in Christ Jesus you who were sometimes far off are made near by the blood of Christ. For He is our peace, who has made both one, and* **has broken down the middle wall of partition between us.** *(KJV)*

Jesus came to undo what Adam and Eve undid in the first place. God created man in His image. He gave him dominion and every advantage that came with being a *friend* of God. After Adam and Eve ate of the tree of knowledge of good and evil, they recognized the sound of God walking in the garden in the cool of the day (Genesis 3:8). In order for them to recognize it, they must have been walking *with* him at some point. Right? That separation, the end of ***that*** type of relationship with God is what Jesus came to restore.

God wants nothing more than to bless you. He will work miracles in your life. But, for a moment, ask not what God can do for you – ask what you can do for God.

God created man to be in a *relationship* with Him. Teaching your children to be a friend of God is much more effective than showing them how to be one of God's groupies. Developing a relationship with God takes time, not unlike our other relationships in life. Hopefully, in your lifetime of making friends and even in meeting your spouse, you haven't been one of those people who take, take, take from relationships, but rather that you are one who balances both giving and receiving.

Paul tells us in Philippians 3:8:

> *Yet furthermore I count everything as loss compared to the possession of the priceless privilege (the overwhelming preciousness, the surpassing worth, and supreme advantage) of* **knowing Christ Jesus my Lord and of progressively becoming more deeply and intimately acquainted with Him.** *(Of perceiving and recognizing and understanding Him more fully and clearly) (Amplified)*

It is vital to our children's faith that we teach them how to become acquainted with God. If your children feel that they only need to seek God when they need help, it is inevitable that they will question their faith at some point. The answers they want will not always be the answers they get. Worse yet, when they don't get the answers they want, they may think that their prayers are going unanswered.

To know God is to be able to recognize and discern what is God and what is not. This is where a progressive relationship comes in.

As your relationship progresses, you will be able

to understand and recognize when God moves in your life. You will see those movements because you are more intimately acquainted with Him. The more you recognize the moves of God in your life, the more you glorify Him rather than taking the glory for yourself. The more you glorify Him, the more He is able to show you.

In 2 Corinthians 3:18, we see how, in the Old Testament, the people did not yet have Christ as their Messiah and there was a barrier that separated the people from God.

> *Whenever though we turn to face God as Moses did, God removes the veil and there we are face to face! We suddenly recognize that God is a living, personal presence, not a piece of chiseled stone. And when God is personally present, a living Spirit, that old constricting legislation is recognized as obsolete. We are free of it! All of us! Nothing between us and God, our faces shining with the brightness of His face. And so we are transfigured much like the Messiah,* ***our lives gradually becoming brighter and more beautiful as God enters our lives and we become more like Him.*** *(The Message Bible)*

When we get to know God and we teach our children how to get to know Him as well, we are more able to trust Him. We recognize that His ways are not our ways, and that His thoughts are not our

To Prepare or To Protect

thoughts.

So, how do we develop this relationship and teach the development process to our children? Well, if your cousin Chet – whom you haven't seen in 20 years – won millions of dollars in the lottery, you would surely not feel comfortable calling him to ask for money. You should feel the same way about asking God for all kinds of things you might not even need without getting to know Him first.

Developing a relationship with God is not a scary, impossible process. Think of it like other relationships you have developed. Here are six steps to developing a relationship with God that have made a huge difference in my life.

Spend time with Him. You can't build a relationship without committing to spend a certain amount of time with Him. When you were dating your spouse, you surely spent a considerable amount of time with that person. I would venture to guess that you would even rearrange your schedule to *make* time for him or her. The same type of commitment needs to be made to God. The more time you spend with Him, the more time you will want to spend.

Increase your intimacy. The intimacy I'm talking about is not physical. It means sharing your dreams, visions and goals. It is important to tell your children they can talk to God about anything. There is nothing too big or too small that God doesn't want to know about you. In these conversations, you may be thanking God for something, telling him a concern or just admiring the beauty in nature that he has provided.

I Peter 5:7 *Casting the whole of you care (all of your anxieties, all of your worries, all your concerns, once and for all) on Him knowing that He cares for you affectionately and cares about you watchfully. (Amplified)*

Develop trust in small steps. Just because you are a Christian doesn't mean you're incapable of failure. It is in our failures that God can show us His faithfulness. Get to know God through His word. Apply a revelation when you receive it, don't just share it with someone else. Celebrate *with* Him when you recognize yourself changing. Acknowledge that *He* was part of the change. Maybe you will start choosing peace, walking in excellence, or overcoming with joy and patience instead of fear and dread. Let Him know how much you appreciate His help. Another way to develop trust with God is to not share everything He reveals to you. Some of the things the Holy Spirit reveals are for you and you alone.

Never have a one-sided relationship with God, based on what you have heard about God. Get to know Him for yourself. If you hear something about God and the way He works that doesn't sit right with you, go to His word and talk to him about it. He will help see you through.

Adapt, change and grow to be the person that fits the relationship. Any successful relationship – whether it is with your spouse, your children or with God – requires us to find a role in that relationship that result in a perfect fit. The only difference in developing a relationship with God is that God does not change. He is the same yesterday, today and forever. So we must adapt *ourselves* to God's way of thinking and submit ourselves even when we don't understand. This is what causes our relationship to grow and mature. Keep in mind that having a relationship with God makes you a part of the body of Christ. You must see your part as special and unique. There is no need to be jealous of anyone else's relationships, gifts or blessings. God's love is freely given to all. *Blessings are a result of obedience to God, not undeserved favor from God.*

Once your relationship is in a more mature place, your thoughts are always on how your choices will affect your relationship with God. God's desires and plans are your number one priority. You learn God's plans through prayer, and you learn His desires by studying His word. Then, you align your life with those plans and desires. Whenever I make tough decisions, I contemplate how those choices will affect my husband and my children. In this same way, we all need to stop and think about how our choices will affect our relationship with God. Never leave God out of the loop when it comes to making decisions.

Once you have reached a place that includes a good solid foundation of faith, trust and reliance on God, life starts getting really good. The more you trust God, the more He can trust you. There is no doubt that God is a big thinker, as exhibited by the multitudes of different people, animals, lands and cultures He has created. Once you have taken the time to get to know God on a more personal and intimate level, you are ready to become a big thinker too.

> John 14:12 *I assure you most solemnly I tell you, if anyone **steadfastly believes** in Me, he will himself be able to do the things that I do; and he will do even greater things than these, because I go to the Father. (Amplified)*

Steadfastly means that you believe consistently, steadily and without wavering. This kind of belief comes from getting to know your heavenly Father on a deeper level than just believing that he exists. We can see through scripture that we *need* to be big thinkers. Jesus tells us what we are capable of, if we can develop this kind of steadfast belief.

> I Corinthians 2:9 *As scripture says, what eye has not seen and ear has not heard and has not entered into the hearts of man (all that) God has prepared (made and keeps ready) for those who love Him. (Who hold him in affectionate reverence promptly obeying Him and gratefully recognizing the benefits He has bestowed.) (Amplified)*

> Ephesians 3:20 *God can do anything, you know – **far more than you could ever imagine or guess or request in your***

To Prepare or To Protect

wildest dreams! He does it not by pushing us around but by working within us, *His Spirit deeply and gently within us. (The Message Bible)*

This is a challenge for us to think bigger. God wants to bless us. He wants us to be big thinkers. Children have no problem thinking big, and generally they have no problem asking for things. So, just like you are responsible for teaching your children proper behavior and manners, you are also responsible for teaching them to develop a proper relationship with God.

Sometimes, we parents are guilty of stifling our children's thoughts and dreams, not realizing just what truly big thinkers they are. As adults, we've been let down in the past because of our lack of faith or lack of relationship with God, so we feel the need to protect our children from this same kind of disappointment.

But if we develop the relationship (and teach our children to do the same), our thinking will be in line with what God would have us think, and our requests will be in line with His will for our lives.

So, allow your children to think big. It comes naturally to them. Your responsibility is to help them develop a relationship that helps all that big thinking yield fruit. God promises to never leave you or forsake you, so imagine Him there waiting for you to call upon His name and start or renew your relationship with him.

Then get ready to think big.

CHAPTER FIVE

Teach them to be Thankful

∞

What if one night, as your family sat down to dinner, one of your children turned to you and said, "Mom and Dad, I just wanted to take a quick minute to say thank you for all that you do for me. I know I sometimes act like I don't appreciate it, and I take advantage of your goodness, but there are not words to express how grateful I am that you are my mother and father. I love you so much. I appreciate the meals you prepare, all the running around you do so that I can enjoy my life, and the awesome way you take care of me. I just had to tell you how much I appreciate you."

Ok, done laughing yet?

I think all parents spend time grousing that our children are unappreciative of all the things we do for them, but we don't stop to realize that thankfulness is a missing component in all our lives. Most of us tend to focus on what we don't have rather than what we do. Too many of us miss the opportunity to usher the very presence of God into our day by being thankful.

We should all ask ourselves when we last told God how much we appreciate Him? If you make thankfulness an everyday practice, you will be amazed at what will happen in your life. God created us in His image and likeness. Thus, just as we like it when people recognize what we do for them, God likes it when we recognize Him.

When you pray with your children, it is important that they see you being thankful and worshipping God, and not just delivering a laundry list of requests you want Him to fulfill.

I can tell you without a doubt that my life did not change until I became thankful. I read and studied the blessings of God and the prosperity promises. I could quote almost every healing scripture, but nothing in my life truly changed until I became thankful.

The reason that teaching your children to be thankful is so important is the very fact that it is not their nature. It is a learned behavior, one that when not taught and not learned will affect their spiritual walk for much time to come. The Bible tells us that the very presence of God is entered through Thanksgiving.

> Psalm 100:4 *Enter his gates with thanksgiving and a thank offering, and into his courts with praise! Be thankful and say so to Him. Bless and affectionately praise*

His name! (Amplified)

Psalm 95:2 *Let us come before His presence with thanksgiving: let us make a joyful noise to Him with songs of praise.* (KJV)

Many Christians lead dry, ineffective prayer lives and then pass that hollowness along to their children. It is vital that they learn to pray effectively. Children have very few problems with faith. They believe God much easier than most adults do. If they are not taught to pray effectively, it can eventually affect their faith.

What do we mean by effective prayer? While God most certainly sees a child's heart and hears all of their prayers, He is not obligated their entire life to simply grant a long list of requests and petitions they bring to the throne. It's a matter of maturing spiritually. Wouldn't it be nice to start them out on the right foot so that they are praying effectively in the baby stage of their spiritual walk, rather than having to learn the hard way like so many of us have had to do?

If you have a difficult time feeling God's presence and you feel as if your prayers are going unanswered, try taking a few days to not ask God for anything. Just reflect on the good in your life. Take the time to tell God about the things for which you are thankful.

During our first few years of marriage, my husband and I didn't have very much. We were incredibly poor. We lived in a mobile home with used furniture and the most awful-looking orange carpeting. At the same time, though, we had more than millions of people around the world had. No matter how hopeless your situation, I promise you there is someone who has it worse. It is all a matter of perspective. No matter how tough things are, there are always reasons to be thankful.

Your children need to see things from the same perspective. People become haughty and self-centered because of lack of thankfulness. Being thankful and having a thankful attitude is a way of showing reverence and awe to God. We certainly must realize that we can't make it in this world without Him.

> I Chronicles 29:11-13 *Yours O Lord is the greatness, and the power, and the glory and the victory and the majesty, for all that is in the heavens and the earth is Yours. Yours is the kingdom O Lord and Yours is to be exalted as Head over all. Both riches and honor come from You and You reign over all. In your hands is power and might: in Your hands it is to make great and to give strength to all.* ***Now therefore our God we thank You and praise Your glorious name and those attributes which that name denotes.*** *(Amplified)*

It's important to take a moment to think about

To Prepare or To Protect

what Jesus went through so that you could have eternal life. You can't read Matthew Chapters 26 through 28 and realize what Jesus endured without feeling tremendous gratitude.

Thankfulness is a way to fight the devil. It shows your submission to God. The book of James tells us that the devil **must** flee when we submit ourselves to God. If you cannot approach God with a thankful heart, you are left to fight too many battles on your own. By not being thankful, you are essentially saying that you need no one.

God requires us to be thankful in **all** things at **all** times. And we shouldn't think that thankfulness is something we can fake. God is no fool. He knows what you need and He knows what you go through. He understands your deepest hurts and desires more than anyone else can. He knows that, at times, our flesh just wants to cry out and not be thankful because we can't see what he sees. Those are the times we must offer our thanksgiving as a sacrifice because it is what God requires and it opens up the very gates to enter into the place where the bigger picture can be revealed.

> I Chronicles 23:30 *They are also to stand every morning to thank and praise that Lord and likewise at the evening.* (Amplified)

> Philippians 4:6 *Do not fret or have anxiety about anything but in **every circumstance** and in everything, by prayer and petition*

(definite requests) **with thanksgiving** *continue to make your wants known to God. (Amplified)*

God does not want you to come begging. He loves you. He wants you to have a calm, cool thankful spirit when you approach him with a need. Jesus exemplifies this for us in the 11th chapter of the book of John. Jesus was about to raise Lazarus from the dead. He started his prayer to God in a spirit of thankfulness.

John 11:41 *So they took away the stone. And Jesus lifted up His eyes and said, "Father,* **I thank you** *that you have heard me."*

The most effective way to help your children have a thankful heart and attitude is to develop one yourself. When you pray with your children, tell God how thankful you are for them, and for all that He does for you. When your children see how much you depend on God, they will not forget. They will be less likely to look to other sources for their needs.

It is a very rare occasion when our children don't begin their prayers with thanking God. Once you have thanked God for things that are on your heart, the petitions that you thought you had may seem very small in comparison to the things God has planned for your life. God reveals Himself and His plans for us through our prayers.

One night not too long ago, our daughter

To Prepare or To Protect

Bridget, said the following blessing over our meal:

> "Dear God, thank you for this food, and thank you that we have enough money to buy what we need. And God thank you that you see the children and the families in Afghanistan and that you know what they need. Amen."

My husband and I both got tears in our eyes at Bridget's understanding of the nature of God. You see she didn't have the answers to the problem and she didn't feel the need to ask for the answer, but she knew that God had the answer. Bridget just let Him know that she was glad that He was in control.

We all need to develop this kind of childlike faith, the kind of faith a thankful heart will give you. We don't always have the answers either when it comes to our children. So, the next time you feel anxious or afraid about your children, thank God that He has a good plan for you and your family. Allow God to be God.

Another way we can help our children have a thankful attitude is to reduce the amount of complaining we do in our lives. Now, since we are human and we do complain as a part of our nature, we will probably never be able to stop completely but we can do a better job of listening to our hearts. If we should burst into a fit of complaining, we need to listen to that little voice inside saying, "there must be something that you can be thankful for...."

Here's an example. Our daughter Chelsie, with

the perfectionist-type personality I discussed earlier, plays basketball in addition to tennis. Because of her perfectionism, she tends to be a little hard on people who don't attend to details the way she does. One day, she was complaining about her basketball practice. She went on and on about the players who don't listen to the coach and don't play their positions correctly. She didn't stop there, she complained that the gym was too cold... you get the picture.

I interrupted her, "Was there anything that happened that you *could* be thankful for?"

She replied, "Yeah, I'm thankful I didn't lose my cool and tell them all off."

Well, that's not exactly what I was shooting for. But, then again, I was also thankful that she didn't tell them all off.

One day, I was out running errands and I had one of those days in which everything that could possibly go wrong certainly did. At dinner that night, I caught myself rattling off my long list of grievances and complaints. Then I stopped myself and said, "But I am so thankful I got everything done, and home in time to have dinner with all of you."

You see, even in your worst moments, you can make a situation better by being thankful. Your children will see the priority you place on a thankful heart and they, in turn, will start exhibiting that kind of behavior. Being thankful is a wonderful way to show your children that you totally rely on God in every aspect of your life. Once these habits are created, they come naturally.

When we are out shopping, if we happen upon a

To Prepare or To Protect

good parking spot, my girls never fail to say, "thank God He gave us another good spot." Once I was working in the kitchen and I dropped a large knife on the floor, just missing my foot by centimeters. Instinctively, I blurted out, "Thank you, Father, that this knife missed my foot."

Life is hard and we are going to make mistake. But being thankful can increase our ability to be empathetic rather than judgmental. We can be patient instead of frustrated, calm instead of anxious, full of faith instead of fear.

And then there are those major moments in life that tell us why thankfulness is so important.

A couple of years ago, as we were moving into our new home, I woke up one morning with very swollen legs. I was short of breath and feeling slightly irritable. I didn't take these symptoms particularly seriously, ascribing them to the pressures of moving, building and trying to figure out how the seven of us were going to live in a two-bedroom apartment until our house was finished.

As the day progressed, though, I didn't feel any better. I'm the kind of person who rarely gets sick; hardly ever even catching a cold, so going to the doctor was not high on my priority list. When the symptoms didn't go away, though, my nursing background helped convince me that I had better go get checked out. Two different doctors examined me. I had an EKG and a chest x-ray. Then, they decided I needed to see a cardiac specialist.

I made an appointment to have an echocardiogram, a test that allows doctors to see the very inner workings of the heart and all its moving parts. It was a week, though, before I could get in to have the test done. While I wasn't really worried, I did start to do a little reflecting on my past. I had tests done when I was 13 for a heart abnormality that was diagnosed as a murmur that I would outgrow. My favorite aunt died suddenly at the age of 34 of a heart defect. At this time, I was 33.

When they day came for my test, I was feeling better and was not feeling very concerned. They ushered me into the room where I was to wait for the technician to administer the test. While I was waiting, I saw my chart laying there and decided to sneak a peek. Under diagnosis were the words, "probably cardiomyopathy." I knew this was not good news. Cardiomyopathy is a severe weakening of the heart muscle. It generally decreases the ability of your heart to continue to function at a pace necessary for the lifestyle of a young mother of five children. The only real course of treatment is a heart transplant.

Even to me, my reaction was odd. By that time, I had been seriously studying the Word for about 10 years, but never before had my faith been tested like this. When I went home that day and had time to think about my situation, I knew that prayer was my first step.

You would think that the natural inclination would be to ask God for healing, especially when I had so much to live for. Somehow, I couldn't bring myself to do it. You see, I believe that God does have a good plan for each and every person and I truly believe that he is in control of every situation.

To Prepare or To Protect

My prayer is still vivid in my mind. I can close my eyes and remember exactly where I was sitting. I can smell the fresh cup of coffee I had just poured myself. I can feel the comfort of my favorite chair, closing my eyes and saying:

> "God thank You for this life You have given me, thank You for the opportunity to learn Your word and teach it to my children. I don't see this illness in Your plan, and I don't believe it is from You. I thank You that by Your stripes I am healed. Yet God I am overwhelmed with thankfulness that my life has changed so much these past few years. I don't want to be sick, but I am prepared for anything as long as You are with me. You have blessed me so much that there is no way that I can see Your hand in this. Thank You that You have a good plan for my family and me. I willingly accept every challenge that comes if it is for Your glory. Thank You because even sickness and the possibility of death could not take away what You have done for me."

I'm not telling you this because I want you to think I am some great pillar of strength or that my faith is something extraordinary. Rather, I want you to know that I learned early on in my Christian walk the importance of being thankful. It is just in me. I know of no other way to pray. Having a background in hospice nursing, I also knew that bad things happen to good people all the time. It is part of living in this world.

Being a thankful person, though, changes your perspective on the world.

It took three days to get the results from my tests. When I called and talked to the cardiologist, he said, "There is absolutely nothing wrong with you, you have the heart of an 18-year-old. Why they sent you in for this test, I don't know."

Misdiagnosis? Maybe, but I think I'll cling to Philippians 4:6.

By teaching your children to be people with a thankful spirit, it will spill over into all areas of their lives. Not only will they be thankful to God, but they will also more quickly recognize and thank others who do good things for them.

My children are always very thankful to their father and I when we do things for them. Anytime we go out to eat or on a family outing, they always thank us. If I run errands for them, they will generally thank me. No, they aren't perfect about this, but they're pretty good.

Sometimes it just amazes me the way some people, especially teens, treat their parents. I tell my children how proud they make me when I see them treat other people so respectfully. It's amusing when our family goes out to a restaurant. Because there are seven of us, the servers will get seven thank-yous when they deliver the drinks, seven more when they bring the food and another seven that come with dessert. If we are still there when they clear the table, they get another seven thank-yous. One time, a waiter told us, "Normally, I don't get this much thankfulness in a whole shift."

What a witness we can be just by being a thankful person. Choose to see the good in all situations. Be a good example to your children. Enter the gates of God with thanksgiving, and watch Him work.

CHAPTER SIX

Character and Integrity are Learned Behaviors

Character and integrity are among the most important attributes we can instill in our children to prepare them for the difficult world in which they must live.

It's not a coincidence that these are also among the most difficult to attain.

The difficulty comes not because of their lack of accessibility, but because of the vagueness of their boundaries. What one may see as a trait of integrity, another may scorn as a right-wing extremist view. Our children are now living in a time in which the definitions of character and integrity are so broad and ill-defined that virtually any behavior can be justified by so-called expert opinions.

This, then, is one area in which we must go to the Word. God has spelled out very clearly what His expectations are for us when it comes to integrity.

In Hebrew, integrity means completeness, uprightness and perfection. Many may become discouraged because we already know that, no matter how hard we try, we cannot be perfect. There's a deeper meaning here, though. As we look closer at the Word, we find that integrity is often referred to as a condition that exists in our hearts. Although our behavior may not be perfect, if our intent is to walk in integrity, we will see that desire displayed in our actions as we mature.

Proverbs 23:7 says, "As a man thinketh in his heart so is he." If we desire to walk in integrity, we will become people of integrity. Because we know that God is perfect, then we can also assume that God **is** integrity. We know, as Christians, that God is always with us and in us and, therefore, we can know that we have the ability to walk in integrity.

It's important to understand what a life of integrity can bring us. Then we can see how critical it is to develop it in our children.

Integrity provides protection, confidence and stability.

> *8 The Lord judges the people; judge me, Lord and do me justice according to my righteousness (my rightness justice, and right standing with you)* ***and according to the integrity that is in me.*** *9 Oh let the wickedness of the wicked come to an end, but establish the (uncompromisingly) righteous (those upright and in harmony with*

*You) for **You who try the hearts and emotions, and thinking powers are a righteous God.** (Amplified)*

David did not have a perfect performance as a human being. Note, though, that the Bible calls David "a man after God's own heart." So we know that David's desire was to do what God wanted him to do and live, as God wanted him to live. Even though he fell short on occasion in the flesh, his heart's desire was to walk in the commandments of God. David also had confidence **with** God. In verse 8, he tells God to "judge me Lord and do me justice according to my righteousness and according to the integrity that is in me."

Now, honestly, how many of us would feel confident enough to tell God to judge the integrity of our hearts? If our hearts seek integrity, then we will have that kind of confidence.

David did not let his imperfect performance stand in the way of having a good heart. He knew that he let God down more than once, just as we all do. He realized, though, that as long as his life was progressing toward becoming the person that he wanted to be, then that person on the inside could still go to God confidently. The old saying, "the spirit was willing but the flesh was weak" applies to all of us just as it did to David.

Integrity and the presence of God

There are scriptures that plainly show us the connection between our desire to walk in integrity and the presence of God we experience in our lives. If you accept this, then you can teach it to your children.

> Psalm 26:7-11 *That I may make the voice of thanksgiving heard and may tell of all Your wondrous works. 8 Lord I love the habitation of Your house, and the place where Your glory dwells. 9 Gather me not with sinners and sweep me not away (with them) nor my life with bloodthirsty men, 10 in whose hands is wickedness and their right hands are full of bribes. 11 But as for me **I will walk in my integrity** redeem me and be merciful and gracious to me. (Amplified)*

Because of David's integrity of heart, he is able to go freely and enjoy God's house and the place where His glory dwells. We know that God dwells in us, and his glory will be there if we learn to walk as David did.

> Psalm 41:12 *And as for me, You have upheld me in my integrity and **set me in Your presence forever.** (Amplified)*

> Proverbs 20:7 *The just man walks in his integrity; blessed (happy fortunate, and to be envied) are his children. (Amplified)*

Your choice to be a person of integrity has a direct affect on your children. None of us as parents

To Prepare or To Protect

would knowingly steal the blessings of our children. God promises that the man who walks in integrity will have blessed children.

As Proverbs 19:1 says, "Better is the poor that walks in his integrity than the rich man who is perverse in his speech and is a self confident fool." Integrity is more valuable than any earthly possession you can acquire.

Now that we've established the importance of integrity and how it affects our lives and our walk with God, let's figure out how we can apply this knowledge on an everyday level and teach it to our children.

I once heard a motivational speaker say, "Character is doing what is right when no one is there to see." Character is carrying out the integrity of your heart and putting it to work through self-discipline. When you are able to do what is right – without recognition, reward, or fear of rejection – then you can consider yourself a person of integrity. If you only do what is right when you know there's something in it for you, one could fairly say that you lack character.

Let's define character as the actions you take to become a person of integrity. There are certain areas that are vital in developing the character-building skills in your children.

Honesty

> Proverbs 6:16-17 *These six things doth the Lord hate; yea seven are an abomination*

*to him. 17 A proud look, **a lying tongue**, and hands that shed innocent blood. (KJV)*

Proverbs 13:5 *A righteous man hates lying: but a wicked man is loathsome and cometh to shame. (KJV)*

Proverbs 26:28 *A lying tongue hates those who it wounds and crushes, and a flattering mouth works ruin. (Amplified)*

These scriptures leave no room for doubt that honesty is vitally important. We've lost touch with that principle in society, becoming more than a little loose with honesty. Too often, we justify the "little white lies" we tell as being harmless.

It is crucial that your children see you as an honest person. There is very little gray area here. The bible makes it clear that GOD HATES A LIAR.

That puts it pretty plainly.

Always stress the importance of honesty. Explaining to your children how a small lie can escalate into something out of control and possibly hurt someone can help them contemplate the consequences of not being truthful. We have told our children from a very young age that we loved them too much to allow them to lie. When we caught them in a lie, it never – and I emphasize the word "never" – went unpunished. They understand the importance of honesty.

Are they honest all of the time? Probably not, but they have seen firsthand the toll lying takes on a

To Prepare or To Protect

young person if they understand the importance of being honest.

Our oldest daughter, Colleen, when she was 14, asked if she could go to a movie with some friends. When I went to pick her up at the theater, neither she nor her friends could be found anywhere. I didn't panic because I knew she was safe in a large group of kids. I asked the theatre staff if there was a problem, or if the movie – one suitable for young people – was running late. They told me everything was fine and that the movie had already let out on schedule.

I went home and told my husband. I was livid because I just knew my child was up to something. He told me not to overreact and just wait to see what Colleen had to say for herself. A little bit later, Colleen called and, in answer to my questions, said there was some trouble with the film and it had run late.

Now, I was really mad since I knew she was lying. Yet, my calm, cool husband said, "Don't react at all. When we pick her up, let's just see how far she decides to go with this." When we arrived at the theater, she was sitting on the curb outside while the rest of her group was still in the theater. She got into the car and burst into tears, telling us, "I don't want to go out for a long time. I think you should ground me for at least a year. I feel terrible. I can't take this. I lied. We went to an R-rated movie. I just want to go home."

Yes, I was disappointed that she had disobeyed us, and yet I had such emotions of relief that what we had taught her about honesty had sunk in. My husband, being the wise man he is, addressed both emotions. He told her he was proud of her for telling the truth, and that she had exhibited maturity by being honest. Then he grounded her and assigned her extra chores around the house for two weeks.

I've overheard my daughter Bridget telling a friend, "I can't lie to my mom because she always seems to know when I am lying." Michelle told a neighbor friend once, "I can't lie to my mom. I think the words liar, liar flash across my eyeballs or something, because whenever I'm lying, mom can tell by looking me in the eyes."

We have a tremendous responsibility as parents to listen and pay attention to our children. When little lies go unnoticed and unpunished, problem lying begins to take root.

Once I heard another mother say that lying is normal in the development of a child. That may be true since we're all born with a sinful nature. However, normal does not necessarily constitute right. Holding your children accountable at a young age for lying will teach them responsibility. They need to know that the choices they make will produce results, good and bad.

Excellence

My childhood was more than a little goofed up, but there is something my parents stressed that I've always carried with me. Both my mother and father would always say, "If you are going to do something, do it right. Give 100 percent and don't do things just halfway."

To Prepare or To Protect

I remember my mother telling me, when I was old enough to start babysitting, that doing a little extra in every job would give me more opportunities to earn money. So when I babysat, I wouldn't just watch the children. I would play with them. I would do the dishes and straighten the house when the children went to bed. I told the people for whom I babysat that I'd be happy to fold their laundry for them, if they wished. Needless to say, I never had a shortage of babysitting jobs and made a pretty good income as a young girl as a result of this principle my parents instilled in me. I've shared this with my girls and they do the same things now that I did then.

Jesus tells us that we should always go the extra mile. He tried to teach the disciples that, as followers of Christ, they should stand out from the crowd. As Christians, we are called upon to be excellent, to stand out from the nonbelievers. This doesn't mean we should be haughty or arrogant, but rather we should live in a way that is enticing to nonbelievers. We should live the kind of lives that makes other people say, "Whatever it is they have, I want it."

We can demonstrate this kind of life to our children by being people who speak excellently, dress excellently, work excellently and live excellently.

We must strive to not just tell the world of God, but also show them the excellence of God. Philippians 1:10 tell us that we must value excellence because others will stumble if we do not.

So that you may surely learn to sense what is vital, and approve and prize what is excellent and of real value. (Recognizing the highest and the best, and distinguishing the moral differences), and that you may be untainted and pure and unerring and blameless (so that with hearts sincere and certain and unsullied, you may approach) the day of Christ (not stumbling nor causing others to stumble) (Amplified)

Going the extra mile means doing more than the average person is willing to do. Since our girls are athletes and musicians, we are continually stressing that being average is not good enough. In order to be excellent, you must be willing to practice just a little bit more than the person you see as being the best does. They may not always follow through, but by sharing this principle they feel a sense of responsibility for the outcome of their chosen activities.

Many parents are afraid to teach their children to be excellent. A lot of the "experts" tell us that it will make our children unbalanced or too driven. When excellence is taught properly, however, it will do just the opposite. You are not teaching your children to be excellent for their own glory, but rather for the glory of God.

Ask yourself this question. Would you like to see your children spending their time working on improving their gifts and talents to their maximum potential? Or rather, spending their time feeling like they are just average and don't really have anything to offer so why bother trying?

Excellence is a state of pursuing something

better. Your children will only go as far in life as they *believe* they can. If you teach them these principles at a young age, they won't settle for being average. They will understand that God has placed within them the seeds of greatness, and that those seeds should be encouraged to grow to their fullest potential.

Excellence is not a matter of trying to be better than everyone else. It is simply you being the best that you can be.

We cannot deny that God himself is excellent. We are God's ambassadors to the world and our children should be God's ambassadors within their circles of influence. I Peter 2:9 tells us that we are "God's own purchased special people set apart to show forth his wonderfulness and perfection." How can we do that if we are not willing to walk in excellence?

Our oldest daughter is the co-captain of her school's varsity basketball team. Their coach has high expectations for this group of girls. His focus for the team is not just to be good athletes, but also good students and good citizens. They dress nicely for all their games, and when they are not in uniform, they are sitting together in the stands cheering for the other squads. Because my daughter has been raised to pursue excellence, she holds this coach in high esteem.

In their handbook, he has placed this quote:

EXCELLENCE

Excellence can be attained...If you
CARE more than others think is wise
RISK more than others think is safe
DREAM more than others think is practical
EXPECT more than others think is possible

We can teach excellence to our children by demanding it of ourselves. Balance your checkbook. Clean out your car. Make your bed. Mow your lawn. Do your laundry from start to finish no more living out of baskets. Treat other people the way you would like to be treated. In fact, take that last one a step further and treat people in a way that would astonish you to be treated.

Speak excellently of others and don't gossip. Be on time and don't leave your house looking like you just rolled out of bed. *If you exemplify excellence, you can expect excellence.* By opting to be mediocre, we do our children a great disservice.

Is achieving excellence hard? You bet it is. Is it worth it? YOU BET! You'll find that your life is simplified and improved by being an excellent person. You will be more organized, have more time and feel better about yourself. Teaching your children these principles when they are young will prepare them for anything that comes their way as adults.

How sad it would be for your children to have to find out later in life what an asset excellent living could be for them, and wonder why *you* never taught them.

Commitment

Today's world pays very little attention to the idea of commitment.

Over 50 percent of married couples wind up divorced. Bankruptcies are at an all-time high. We see billions of dollars worth of lawsuits being filed. These are all examples of a lack of commitment in today's society.

Your children need to see in you an example of commitment.

The key to being able to stay committed is separating yourself from your flesh. You see, the flesh is always weak and wants only what feels good. Commitment is doing what you said you would do even when you don't feel like it. When the urge to break a commitment comes, we can't consult with our flesh. Instead, we need to consult the Holy Spirit. No one ever said life is easy. Life is more rewarding, though, when we honor our commitments.

There aren't many married couples who don't wonder at some point if their lives would have been better had they not made the decision to marry who and when they did. For me, being married at 18 and having five children by the age of 25 was definitely a good way to find out what kind of stuff you're made of in the commitment department.

We find everyday how important commitment is in our lives. How many parents have had children, and then given up on them when things got tough? By the same token, how many Christians made their commitment to turn their life over to Christ only to be lead by their feelings and desires back to their former way of living? Being committed means sticking with the big things and the small, be it an exercise program, a diet or your commitment to your children.

Being 18 years old, a senior in high school and pregnant, I was forced to think about commitment at an early age. After I told Mike that I was pregnant, he suggested that we get married. When I was a little girl, all I ever really wanted to do was get married and have a family, but I also knew that I wanted to get married only once. Being pregnant in our family was bad enough. I would already be branded for life. Divorce would simply not be an option, even though the odds would be against us.

The more we talked about it, the more I believed we could do it. We told each other that divorce would never be a viable choice for us.

Well, we didn't live a fairy tale life at the beginning. My poor husband had no idea what he had gotten himself into when he married his high school sweetheart who brought her own emotional baggage into the marriage. I bet he thought about divorce at least hundreds of times in the first five years we were married.

He may have thought about it, but he never mentioned it.

As hard as times were for us, I can't recall a single conversation in which we entertained the idea of getting divorce. Please understand, I do realize there are circumstances in which divorce must take place in order to protect the safety and well-being of one or both of the people involved, but that's not the

To Prepare or To Protect

case in the 53 percent of marriages that end in divorce.

Mike and I could have easily been divorced and justified it, and people would have accepted it as the inevitable result of marrying so young. Now that we have been married 18 years, though, we can look back and laugh and realize that the joy was in the struggles – not just enduring them, but overcoming them.

When you give up on a commitment, it usually means one of two things. You made an emotional decision without thinking it through completely, or you thought your decision through but you're not willing to see it through. Commitment requires you to *think it through, and then see it through.*

Our daughter Chelsie plays the piano. She picked it up very quickly and, after just a short period of taking lessons, she was able to play very entertaining music. Soon, her two sisters decided they, too, wanted to take piano lessons. We told them what would be required of them. They would not be allowed to quit lessons until they had taken them for at least three years. They would be expected to practice regularly. And we stressed that, no matter how hard it was or how long it takes to master a song, you must see it through to the end. Quitting would simply not be an option.

Anyone who has a child in piano lessons knows there will be a time in which they will simply no longer want to practice or go to lessons. When that day comes, it will be tempting to look at the dollars and time you'll save by letting them quit. As a parent, though, you must stay committed and make your child stick to the path they've chosen.

There's a reason we make our children stick to their lessons for three years. Did you realize that about 75 percent of all divorces happen before the third year of marriage? My girls have wanted to quit piano lessons because they thought they would sound like Mozart after just a few lessons, but they don't realize what they would be giving up if they quit because of their initial frustrations. If I had walked away from my marriage when things didn't go exactly as I wished, I would have given up the greatest part of my life and would never have realized what I had lost.

Reading this, you may be wondering how I can possibly compare a marriage to piano lessons. In both instances, though, commitment is involved. My girls were told before they began piano lessons that it would be hard. They made the choice to commit, knowing what would be involved for them. My responsibility as a parent is to help them see it through.

(This is why, by the way, all good churches require premarital classes so that engaged couples can clearly understand what they are getting into, before they make the commitment.)

Don't allow your children to get in the habit of making loose commitments. When they do this, they are being led by their emotions and feelings and it will give them lifelong problems. As James 1:8 tells us, "A double-minded man is unstable in *all* his ways." Not sticking to commitments is exactly the thing that develops double-mindedness.

To set a good example, we parents cannot be quitters.... in anything. If we take the time to make good quality commitments, we will demonstrate to our children the importance not only of staying committed but also the importance of patience and self-discipline. Because children and teens are predominately led by their emotions, parents must help them think issues through completely. Ask them questions and give them examples of who will be hurt if they don't see through their commitments. Make them think, and then hold then accountable.

By making good decisions, you will instill in them a quality that will save them future heartache in their lives. And, after all, isn't that what being an ambassador of God is all about?

Empathy

Most people don't have a clear understanding of the meaning of empathy. Empathy is the ability to put yourself in someone else's place – to understand why they do what they do, act like they act, or think like they think.

Empathy is important. It plays a major role in teaching your children to not judge others, to not be offended by others and to be patient with those they encounter in their lives. Being able to put yourself in someone else's shoes makes you a more compassionate person. It will also cause you to be blessed.

Probably a lot of you are like I was. I was very empathetic. The only problem was that the person with whom I was empathetic was *myself*. I could justify every single one of my tantrums, fits and other examples of obnoxious behavior, but I had no tolerance for anyone else's. If this describes you, it's critical to get past this state of being and move to a higher level. Empathy allows you to see the good in others. It helps you to understand that when people hurt you, sometimes it is simply because they are hurting.

Empathetic people make the world a better place for all of us. And, somehow, my children have developed their sense of empathy to a point I can only hope to achieve one day. I know God has worked in them, and I see examples of this constantly. Let me give you a few examples of empathy at work.

- My youngest daughter, nine-year-old Molly, almost always sees the best in every person she encounters. One day, she came home from school uncharacteristically sad. She told me about a little boy who had been very disruptive that day, both in class ad on the playground. She told me it saddened her because this same little boy was constantly getting into trouble to the point that the teachers were even saying mean things to him.

    She said, "Once, he said his mom was coming to have lunch with him, and she didn't come. I think people should be nice to him, because his mommy is not nice to him. She told him she didn't want him anymore. If more people would be nice to him, he probably wouldn't be naughty."

Then she said the sweetest thing, saying simply, "I feel so bad for him that I think my heart hurts.

- Bridget was 13 and in junior high. One day at school, she noticed a boy who spoke with broken English standing under a stairwell as students shuttled through the halls between classes. She said she had seen him there day after day, so she made it a point of walking over to him and starting a conversation. She learned that he liked to wait under the stairs until most of the kids had cleared the halls, because he had apparently been the victim of some not so kind-hearted boys.

  The next day, Bridget took some of her friends with her to introduce them to this young boy. They invited him to sit with them at lunch, and made it a point to offer a friendly hello whenever they saw him. In just a week, he began to make friends with some other boys in the 7th grade and no longer had to wait under the steps between passing periods. She said, "He's a very nice boy. We just needed to get the ball rolling for him. I think he just needed a little confidence booster."

- Once my oldest daughter and I were in a department store picking up a couple of things she needed for school. Trying to find the shortest checkout line, we noticed an elderly gentleman engaged in a similar search. He was apparently upset at the ratio of patrons to checkers, because he was moving from lane to lane and cussing as he went.

He was behind us in line when the cashier needed to change the tape in her register. This prompted him to let loose with a barrage of words not appropriate for the time, the situation, or this book. After his outburst, he stomped away to the return counter.

As we stood in line, I watched him. He was about 5'6" and almost as round as he was tall. He had a visible scowl over sad eyes, and his body language conveyed an air of fatigue. He was probably in his late 60's or early 70's. He thought he could circumvent the checkout lines by paying for his goods at the return counter, but I knew from experience that the clerk there was going to send him right back from whence he came.

I could not hear the exchange of words, but I could see his agitation as he picked up his box of shoes and stormed away. As the man made his way back to the checkout area, a cashier opened a register in the lane next to ours and said, "I can help people over here." Colleen was paying for her purchases with her own money so she went to the new lane just as the elderly man was doing the same. The man was obviously upset that Colleen had moved into this line ahead of him, even though she was oblivious to his return. I watched him as he bolted toward her with the shoebox over his head as if he was going to hit her with it.

I wasn't so worried about Colleen. She is 5'8" and athletic, and my worry was that she would pound this little man in self-defense if he tried to assault her with his shoebox. Because his approach was announced by another barrage of obscenities, he caught her attention. What she did next amazed me.

She looked right into his eyes, smiled a great big smile and said, "I'm so sorry. I didn't see you." The cashier had already rung up her item on the register. Otherwise, I'm convinced she would have let him go ahead of her. He didn't hit her with the shoes, but instead slammed them on the belt and continued to grumble under his breath. As we walked out of the store, I started in, "Can you believe that guy. What an unbelievable display...."

Colleen interrupted me and said, "Mom, maybe this was the first time he's been out since his wife died or something. He looked so sad. Why don't you cut him some slack?" I was so proud of her – not to mention embarrassed for myself – that I almost cried.

Children have a natural ability to be kind and compassionate. We adults, by contrast, have experiences and emotions that cloud our ability to put ourselves in other people's shoes. The best way to teach your children empathy is to tell them about it, work as hard as you can to develop it in yourself, and then watch them go and learn from them.

I don't like saying this, but I think sometimes that we Christians are the guiltiest of a lack of empathy. We sometimes tend to think that we have it all together, especially when we compare ourselves to those who do not believe as we do. It is too easy for us to judge and condemn. The hard reality, though, is that we are not supposed to compare ourselves to nonbelievers.

Instead, we are supposed to use Jesus as our standard. Jesus is not as impressed by your spiritual status as you think he is. He said himself that he didn't come to save the righteous, but rather to seek and save the lost. In fact, Jesus makes it clear to us in Matthew 7 what we should do when judgmental thoughts come into our minds.

> *1 Do not judge and criticize and condemn others, so that you may not be judged and criticized and condemned yourselves. 2 For just as you judge and criticize and condemn others, you will be judged, criticized and condemned, and in accordance with the measure you use to deal out to others it will be dealt out again to you. 3 Why do you stare at the very small particle that is in your brother's eye but do not become aware of and consider the beam of timber in your own eye? 4 Or how can you say to your brother, "Let me get the very tiny particle out of your eye, when there is a beam of timber in your own eye?" 5 You hypocrite first get the beam out of your eye*

and then you will see clearly to take the tiny particle out of your brother's eye. (Amplified)

Furthermore, Galatians 6:1 says:

*Brethren if any person is overtaken by misconduct or sin of any sort, you who are spiritual (who are responsive to and controlled by the Spirit) should set him right and restore him **without any sense of superiority and with all gentleness and meekness. Keeping an attentive eye on yourself lest you should be tempted also.** (Amplified)*

It is vitally important that we teach our children to be empathetic toward others, Christian and non-Christian alike. Empathy allows us to admit that "but for the grace of God, there go I."

When I pray for my children, I make it a point to pray that they see people through the eyes of God and see them as God sees them. I also pray this for myself when I pray with my children.

Allow me to offer one additional suggestion. Include a prayer to help you deal with the heaviness that comes from seeing what God sees. God sees people who are hurting, who are in physical and emotional pain. If God deals mercifully with us, then shouldn't we think and expect that he would do the same with others, particularly those in anguish? Help your children to see people in an empathetic way. It will help them to change the world around them and make this a better place for all of us.

Submission

The word "submission" is one of the most misunderstood in the English language and, consequently, can cause a stir in just about any discussion group.

If you ask any number of people what they think submission means, the vast majority would say it is some kind of oppression or belittlement. Only a very few would tell you that submission is one of the most powerful assets we have in living a successful life.

Webster's Dictionary defines submission as "to yield or defer to the opinion or authority of another." Submission is no more a state of weakness than domination is a state of strength. When we teach our children to submit to authority, we have given them the ability to truly learn and expand their thought process. To submit is to realize that, in order to accomplish anything, we must put our own opinions aside and open our minds to the thoughts of those who have something to offer to us. Generally, those to whom we submit have our own best interests at heart.

Let me make this clear. Submission does not mean that our own opinions are unworthy. It simply means that we are willing to lay our opinions aside to accomplish a desired goal.

I can't begin to count the number of times I refused to back down to my husband, pushing and demanding and fighting until he would finally throw up his hands and say, "Okay, have it your way." Then, matters would blow up in my face because I

To Prepare or To Protect

wouldn't listen to him. I have to give my husband a lot of credit. In his desire to keep peace, he let me mess up a lot of things. When it came to important issues, though, he always stood his ground.

While this book is about children, I need to share with you a valuable story regarding submission to my husband because it does have something to say about family life.

As I said, my husband has always been a very peaceful person and he knew that I was, in no way, going to allow him to dominate me. I would throw these obnoxious fits to get my way and, more often than not, he would give in. There were times I thought he didn't fight hard enough for what he wanted, but he would always say, "I'm not going to stand here and have a shouting match with you. Just do whatever you want."

One day, when our three oldest girls were very small, I was ranting and railing on them over something so trivial I don't even remember what it was. The girls were crying, and their tears just fueled my rage all the more. Mike came into the room, looked calmly at me and said, "I have had enough of this. You are completely out of control. I absolutely will not have you screaming at these kids like this. This is my house, and if you want to live here you will not raise your voice like that ever again. I don't want to hear it anymore. I have put up with as much as I can. If you cannot control yourself, there is the door." Then he gathered up the girls, turned and walked away.

Normally, I would have let him know right then

and there what I thought. But, at that moment, I knew he meant what he said. I had pushed him to the point of no return. While I can't say that I've never raised my voice since then, I will say that it was a long time before I did and I'm quick to apologize whenever I do.

You see, my husband was raised in a very peaceful home. His parents didn't yell at each other or their children. There were disagreements, but yelling never solved them. By contrast, I grew up in a home where the only way we communicated was to yell and argue about everything. Battles were nonstop, and nothing was ever really solved. Arguments ended in fits of frustration and discouragement.

The point is this. My husband had something very valuable to offer me, something that would greatly improve my own life. The only way, though, that I could attain what he was offering was to put my own feelings and way of doing things aside and submit to his way of doing things. That day, I probably could have packed a bag and left. I am very certain he would have let me go. Then, I would have lived my life raising my children on alternate weekends and holidays, and my youngest two children would never have been born. I would have wallowed in self-pity, seeing myself as a victim and living out the rest of my days angry and bitter.

By submitting to my husband, I change the course of the rest of my life. There is rarely a day I don't think about that incident and thank God for giving me such a tremendous husband. I also thank Him for keeping me from making the biggest mistake of my life.

Scripture has a lot to say about submission. The world will deliver a lot of messages on the subject that may feel more comfortable to you, but it necessary for us to discover the truth about submission for the well-being and development of our children. Keep in mind again that submission is not synonymous with being a doormat. It takes much more strength and intestinal fortitude to lay your own personal opinions and ways of doing things aside for the sake of unity, order, wisdom and blessing than it does to pitch a fit to get your way.

Ephesians 5:21 tells us, "Submit yourselves one to another in the fear of the Lord." This is saying that *all* of us at sometime will need to submit to someone else out of respect to God. Fear in this verse refers to reverence, or respect for God's desires. Whether it is to keep peace, show honor or accomplish a goal is not the central issue. What's important is that we must all submit to one another at sometime. Nothing in this world is ever accomplished unless people learn to submit.

James 4:7 *Submit yourselves to God resist the devil and he will flee from you. (KJV)*

Submitting to God is powerful spiritual welfare. It means doing what He says to do, even if we don't agree or understand. We're told, for example, to pray for those who persecute us, to love our enemies, to turn the other cheek. Submitting means doing these things without debate or argument because we know

God has our best interests at heart. Just as my husband had our children's and my best interests at heart, you want to scream that it's not fair but you submit yourself and watch the blessings come.

One way we can teach our children the power of submission is to submit ourselves to God and to other authorities.

> I Peter 2:13-14 *Be submissive to every human institution and authority for the sake of the Lord whether it be emperor as supreme or to governors as sent by him to bring vengeance punishment justice to those who do wrong and to encourage those who do good service. (KJV)*

We don't have to agree with every law or rule adopted by our governments and social institutions, but we do our children and ourselves a huge disservice if we don't abide by them. Like it or not, rules are ***not*** made to be broken. Your submission is twofold when you abide by laws and rules with which you don't agree. First, you're submitting to the law that you choose to obey and, second, to God because he tells you to do it. If you feel unfairly treated, then you should appeal to God, turn it over to Him and trust Him to take care of the problem.

It is vital that we don't cheat the system, so that we don't allow our children to think that we are above the rules. Some rules may make absolutely no sense to us, but that does not give us the right to disobey them.

To Prepare or To Protect

When our children were small, we took them to a movie and my husband wanted me to get one of my big purses and stuff it full of snacks to have in the theater. I told him I didn't feel right doing this because of the signs posted in the lobby saying "no outside snacks allowed in the theater." While I don't think it would be a federal crime to bring some snacks to the movies, the example we would set for our children may well be a small start to a dangerous pattern.

If this story seems insignificant to you, think of how many large problems in society began with a small incident. It is very dangerous to teach your children that they can pick and choose which rules they will submit to, and which they will not. We're living in a time in which too many people believe there is no absolute truth and that individuals must choose for themselves what is right for them. This philosophy can only lead to chaos.

While I most certainly do not agree with everything that has happened in our government in the last few years, I still realize that this is the greatest nation in the world and that it was founded on Godly principles. We need to teach our children that the power of submission can change things for the better. Submitting to God, to authorities and even submitting to rules we don't understand will give them a powerful weapon for a war that is not fought by carnal weapons.

Respect
"Respect the noun."

That's a phrase my husband has used with our children since they were young. "Respecting the noun" means showing respect to any person, place or thing. It's a philosophy sorely lacking in our society today.

It saddens me when I go out shopping and see the incredible amount of disrespect that people show to one another. Teaching respect is vital to our children's long-term success. Our children need to learn the basics like looking into people's eyes when they speak, saying please and thank you, picking up their trash, putting their things away, offering a helping hand when they are a guest in someone's home. These are just a few of the things that all of us should be doing on a regular basis to offer a good example to our youth.

When I was young, if someone asked me a question and I didn't answer them in a complete and polite sentence, I was sure to get some sort of punishment from one of my parents. Yet today, when you go to a counter in a fast food restaurant, you're lucky to get much more than a grunt and a blank stare from the person behind the register.

So many people blame youth for the changes that have taken place in our society. It never ceases to amaze me when I listen to adults complain about the disrespectful way kids behave "these days." Did we suddenly start giving birth to mutant babies incapable of being respectful? Of course not. All behaviors other than the fear of falling and the fear of loud noises are learned. Children may be more disrespectful than we were when we were kids, but they had to have learned that disrespectfulness from somewhere.

We must take it upon ourselves to show respect to others. Jesus said that we should do unto others, as we would have done unto us. What kind of a world would this be if people only practiced that one commandment? When I was a little girl, my dad used to tell us at the beginning of every school year, "I know that you will probably not get straight A's and that is okay. Occasionally, you may even get into a little scuffle on the playground, and that's understandable. One thing that had better not ever happen is for me to find out you disrespected your teacher."

That has stuck with me my entire life and I've passed it on to my own children. It is important that they know that they don't always have to agree with teachers, pastors or even me, but that they will treat people with respect. Can you imagine how much better our schools would be today if every parent taught their children this lesson?

How do you teach a child respect? It takes more than just good examples. In addition to being a person of respect yourself, you must make a conscious decision to train your children to be respectful. This is not easy. None of us are born with a respectful nature. We are all born into sin. It takes continuous effort and a tenacious attitude to adhere to a respectful nature.

Sometimes, parents think they are being too hard on their children if they command respect, but a loose attitude about teaching your children to be respectful will cause more unhappiness in the long run. You must be a person of vision to raise children, not living from moment to moment just doing what is easy. You must see your children's futures before they do. At times, you will have to punish, rebuke and correct them, just as God does you.

It may be hard, but it comes with a reward.

For some of us, sticking to an exercise program is hard, but we eventually reap the rewards from it and it becomes easier and even enjoyable. The same is true with parenting. There are things that are hard, and being consistent is one of them. Your children will develop a trust and respect for you, even though they may not see it now. When they are adults, you will be their model for good parenting.

The next time your child acts out and you try to correct them to no avail, then correct them again.... and again.... and again...and again. At some point, you're going to think to yourself, "oh, just forget it, it's not worth the battle." But it IS worth the battle. In fact, the battle is necessary. Children are not stupid. They choose their battles based on victories. You are not doing the wrong thing when you correct your child. Rather, you are teaching them the principles they need to have a better, more successful life.

You will literally see your children's attitudes change before your eyes. I wish I could say there comes a time when you will never have to go nose-to-nose with your children, but there isn't. As they get older, though, they begin seeing things in a different light and they understand better all that you have done for them. They will thank you for taking the time to "command respect" because you have given them something so valuable. When their teachers, coaches and friends' parents praise them for their tremendous attitudes, work ethics and character, they will understand exactly what you did for them. When the so-called experts tell you that children need to explore their personalities and express their feelings, always remember that children do not think like adults, yet that is what they are on the road to becoming. It is your responsibility as parents to train your children up in the way they should go.

You are not going to alter their personalities by teaching them to be people of character and integrity; you are going to enhance them.

Respecting people is not a weakness. It is a strength and part of the foundation that builds a person of character and integrity. Our children need to know that what they sow they will also reap, and if they sow seeds of disrespect they will someday reap the same. If they sow seeds of unity and respect, then that is what they shall reap in their futures.

Honesty, excellence, commitment, empathy, submission and respect are critical in building character and integrity in your children. By relying upon these touchstones, you will see your children develop into young people of great character and you will not be disappointed. As they grow and develop, you will watch them in joy and amazement and then you will thank God because they will not have the more difficult task of learning these concepts as adults through the clouds of life and past experiences.

They, in turn, will thank you when they realize

the course of their lives was affected by the time and energy you devoted to instill and expect these basic principles and behaviors. They will be prepared to meet head-on all of the challenges and difficulties from which you've wanted to protect them.

In all of this, God will be glorified through you to your children and for generations to come.

CHAPTER SEVEN

The Pharisee Factor

More than anything, children need to see the goodness of God through their parents. In this chapter, we're going to ask ourselves just how well we're displaying that goodness. Parents are, in a sense, God's ambassadors to their children. It's a rewarding responsibility. Watching the principles of God develop in your children has got to be the most moving thing for a parent to witness. Next to the actual moment that each of my daughters was born, seeing them grow and develop into young women of character and integrity with a love and trust in God is the aspect of my life that motivates me the most.

The sad thing is that there are millions of well-meaning, God-fearing, churchgoing people who miss this rewarding experience. They read all the books, follow all the charts, memorize all the rules and still muddle through hoping that their children turn out all right. In many of these cases, the problem is that their children are onto them.

You see, children are very spiritually discerning. They can recognize a hypocrite a mile away. That's probably because they are frequently on the receiving end of hypocrisy. They see too many adults in their lives that talk a good game without actually living one. There is a great country music song entitled, "I'd Rather See a Sermon Than Hear One Any day" and it contains lyrics that include, "I'd rather watch them walk with me than to merely show the way."

There's a lot of truth in that song. How many of our children hear adults telling them how to live the right kind of life, and then see them living their own lives by an entirely different set of rules?

I remember, as a child, my family going to church every single Sunday. We belonged to a very traditional denominational church. Now, there are a lot of fine denominational churches, but this one was as frigid as the North Pole. I saw the same people meeting in the church basement every week and watch them gossiping, backbiting, grumbling, murmuring and complaining over their juice and donuts. There were divorces, affairs and hypocrisy aplenty.

Even within my own family, there would be fussing and arguing all the way to church, and then all the way back home. We would get punished as children if we used profanity, but then we saw every grownup in authority cussing to a degree that would put a sailor to shame. When I turned 18, I was actually kicked out of the church for confronting the pastor on the issue of walking in love. It's a good

To Prepare or To Protect

story that I'll return to a little later in this chapter.

Suffice to say, though, that my own church experience as a teenager didn't provide me with a very good revelation of what God was like. That brings me to the thrust of this chapter, something I like to call "the Pharisee factor."

In Matthew 23, Jesus says "Woe unto you scribes and Pharisees" not just once, but six times. Woe is an expression of extreme grief or disappointment. You see, Jesus was impressed with the amount of law the Pharisees knew, but he was very unimpressed with their ability to put that knowledge to use. These Pharisees may have been suffering from the same kind of "information constipation" we discussed earlier in this book. They had all kinds of information, rules and regulations to follow, but they lacked the wisdom to put them to proper use. What caused this problem? More than likely pride, wrong motivations, laziness and haughtiness were the culprits.

Many of us as parents suffer from the same factors that caused the Pharisees so much trouble. We as parents are the spiritual leaders of our children – just as the Pharisees were the leaders of the church in their day – and we need to determine if we are as ineffective as the Pharisees were.

In order to determine if you're suffering from the Pharisee Factor, you need to be willing to drop your emotional defenses and take a long, deep look at yourself. This can be painful, especially if you're as confused and stubborn as I was. Think of this as something similar to labor pains. It may seem almost unbearable at times, but the end result will provide a level of joy that far exceeds the pain. If you follow the process, there will be a reward at the end of the pain. If you continue on the path of not seriously looking at yourself, you're simply setting yourself up for a very LONG labor with no joy at the end. Your children will simply grow up and go out into the world, with you telling yourself you did the best you could and crossing your fingers.

God promises in Deuteronomy 28 that *if we listen diligently to the voice of the Lord our God, and be watchful to do all His commandments.... BLESSED shall be the fruit of your body!* The fruit in this case is our children, but we can't listen diligently and be watchful to do His commandments if we don't know them.

Ok, let's walk through this self-examination step by step. And, remember, I've got some qualification as a guide here because I was once a Pharisee myself – not only with my children, but with my husband, my neighbors, friends, relatives and any unfortunate stranger who happened into my path. Jesus is very clear regarding these problems with the Pharisees in Matthew 23, so let's dissect that chapter as we engage in a little critical self-examination.

> *4. They tie up heavy loads, hard to bear and place them on men's shoulders, but they themselves will not lift a finger to help bear them.*

In these words, we see that the Pharisees place high expectations on people to perform, knowing all the while that no human being is perfect and that those expectations would be unattainable. The finger that should have been lifted may have been referring to mercy and encouragement, and maybe a little exhortation.

Do you sometimes place expectations on your children to perform in a certain way, maybe even in a way that emulates success you've had in your life? Let's dig a little deeper. Do you place expectations on your children to behave a certain way, and then don't even place those same expectations on yourself? Or, do you place unreachable expectations on them and yourself and then live in frustration because none of you are measuring up to your standards?

The problem lies not in placing expectations on your children. I have extremely high ones for my children, but they are exactly that – expectations and goals that are high but attainable with work, help, encouragement and cooperation. They are not impossible dreams.

The Pharisees saw themselves as perfect and everyone around them as just shy of that mark. People do this to their children every day without even realizing it. Believe me, your children can sense it if you feel they aren't measuring up. Don't stop setting expectations for your children, but lift a finger to show them the way. And, most important of all, **don't expect more of them than you are willing to offer in example.** I often like to say, what you do speaks so loudly that they can't hear what you say.

For example, when you tell your children that lying is wrong, you have to mean it. Don't let your children hear you telling a telemarketer that you already have the product he's selling just so you can get him off the phone. Don't ask your children to tell someone you are not available when you are. And never, never use the excuse that certain behaviors are okay for you, but not for your children, because you are an adult.

Nothing will make a child resent a parent more than the persistence of hypocrisy. My children still occasionally hit me with this one when they feel I am judging people. After all, I'm very quick to correct them when I feel they are judging someone for any reason. If I say something about someone that comes across as even slightly judgmental, my children will tell me, "mom, judge not lest ye be judged." I stand embarrassed, but also relieved that my children recognize the dangers of being this way.

5 They do all their works to be seen of men.

This is so important to me, because I was so guilty of it myself. I used to make certain my children behaved everywhere we went (and they knew they had better behave....or else), but I demanded it for all the wrong reasons. I was not making them behave so that they could receive the praise for their good behavior, or because I wanted to glorify God. No, I wanted them to behave so that I would look good. I wanted my children to serve as prima facie evidence that **I** was a good parent.

We all need to examine the motivations behind

our actions. Do we volunteer for activities to make ourselves look good in the eyes of others, and then complain incessantly and make our families suffer because we don't want to follow through on our commitments? Do we overbook ourselves, and then resent having to spend time on duties for which we have no desire? If you are guilty of these things, then don't expect your children to behave differently.

Jesus addresses the emphasis the Pharisees place on the titles they hold. We should ask ourselves which of our titles make us the most proud. When you visit with a stranger who asks you what you do, how do you answer and what is your heart saying? When I'm asked what I do, a lot of things come to mind. I do laundry. I read books. I drive my car. These activities mean as much to me as any fancy title. It is important that we do not instill in our children that any one person is more important or more valuable than anyone else, simply because of a title.

God is no respecter of persons, and he loves all people regardless of their title. If your children see that you value a title more than the actual person, they will do the same. And they may feel driven to find that kind of title themselves. They will fail to realize that God said, "The greatest among you shall be your servant."

How do you avoid this problem with your children? An important starting point comes in not comparing your children to one another, or comparing your only child to other children. We, as parents, must see the good in each child, and recognize each child's individual gifts.

Our first two daughters had a very easy time with school. They started well from day one and continue to be predominately "A" students. Our third daughter, though, struggled with school every step of the way. She didn't like to go. She hated to read, and she absolutely despised math. I used to say to her, "Don't you want to get A's like Colleen and Chelsie?" She would be quite emphatic in responding, "No."

Each time we had this discussion, I could see the hurt in her eyes when I emphasized the good grades her sisters were getting. Finally, I had the revelation that I was communicating to her that she was less important because she didn't get A's. While I was criticizing her for her grades, I wasn't mentioning the fact that her teachers always praised her good behavior, her work ethic and hear ability to befriend every single, lonely child in class.

I was so ashamed and saddened by my own behavior, realizing that I had a serious Pharisee problem on my hands. I apologized to her and told her I was so sorry that I hadn't been noticing all of the great things she was doing. I told her that what mattered was that she continued to work hard and do her absolute best, and that I was proud of her efforts.

This exchange occurred when she was in fourth grade. By sixth grade, she had become a straight "A" student. Now, she loves school. Her number one priority, though, is not her grades, and they aren't my priority either. She said to me one day, "I just want to be the best me I can be."

And that's just fine with her mother.

To Prepare or To Protect

> Matthew 23:10 *13 Woe to you scribes and Pharisees, pretenders, (hypocrites) For you shut the kingdom of heaven in men's faces for you neither enter yourselves nor do you allow those who are about to go in to do so.*

This is one of the Pharisees' most dangerous activities. Jesus was greatly upset by the incredible religiousness the Pharisees continually exhibited. Until Jesus arrived on the scene, the Pharisees were the spiritual leaders of the land, but Jesus' message to them was clear.

He said, "God loves you. He loved you enough to send Me here to die for the sins of the world. All He asks is that you believe it and receive Me. Love God enough to trust this message, abide in Me and We will abide in you. After I have accomplished my work here, I will go back to be with the Father, then I will send the Holy Spirit and He will lead you and guide you. I will be here living in you, so you will not need to fear the evil one. I am going to defeat him once and for all. When I say it is finished, it will be. You will become one with me and I will dwell in you and we will walk out this human experience together."

You can imagine what the Pharisees thought of this school of thought. It was inconceivable to them, because they believe in a covenant made up of works and sacrifice. Entering the kingdom of heaven, to a Pharisee, means a never-ending series of works – a trip that is full of religious tradition that is not necessarily scriptural. Sadly, though, most people who behave like Pharisees or are the victims of those who do don't realize that this behavior is not scriptural because they don't seek the answers for themselves.

Yet, the answer is clear to us in Mark 10:15, which tells us, "Truly I tell you, whoever does not receive and accept and welcome the kingdom of God like a little child (does) positively not enter it."

Jesus said, In Matthew 23:13, that the Pharisees shut the kingdom of heaven in men's faces. You see, we naturally want to believe that Jesus loves us. We want what God wants, and we want it to be easy. The Pharisees, though, want you to believe that this easiness is just too good to be true. If you are a Pharisee, then you believe the kingdom of God is still going to be works, sacrifice, penance and lack of faith. If we dig deeper, though, we will find that:

> *The kingdom of God is not meat and drink, but righteousness, and peace, and joy in the Holy Ghost. Romans 10:14 (KJV)*

Jesus died to give you *this* kind of kingdom. In the book of John, He said that He came so that we would have and enjoy our lives, and that we would have joy overflowing. Is that your life? Do you have joy overflowing? If you don't, who will show your children how to discover that joy?

I had my own eye-opening experiences with the religious Pharisees. I was raised in a traditional church, knew that God was real, and wanted desperately to believe that He loved me. In the lives of

To Prepare or To Protect

---

those around me, though, there was no apparent evidence of the joy to be found in God's love. We weren't completely miserable, but we certainly weren't exhibiting a joy unspeakable.

I always had an empty void in me that I just knew had something to do with God or, more specifically, the barriers my church placed between God and I. Not only couldn't I find the missing piece in my heart, but I wasn't even allowed to look for it. I was told that I couldn't read the Bible because I couldn't possibly understand it...and, besides, Bible reading was reserved strictly for those in church leadership. We were allowed to read only prewritten prayers and books provided to us by our religion.

Once I asked my dad why I couldn't simply talk to God in my own words. I thought he was going to have a stroke. He thought I needed to be exorcised for such blasphemy.

I waited patiently until my 18th birthday, having always been the recipient of the speech at home that went, "As long as you live in my house, you will abide my rules and when you turn 18, you can do whatever you want." Well, as soon as I turned 18, I made an appointment with the leader of our church to ask him some questions that had been on my mind for years. I felt certain that I would come away from this meeting with a renewed and better understanding of my relationship with God.

These questions came in rapid-fire succession. If God is love and you are supposed to be the representation of God, why are you so cruel to me? Why do you shut me up every time I try to ask you a question?

Why don't we invite people from outside the congregation to visit our church? Shouldn't we be concerned about helping those who don't know God?

Our meeting lasted about 15 minutes. It ended with him telling me very bluntly that I was possessed by demons and was destined for an eternal life of damnation.

Things, in other words, didn't go quite as I had planned.

I was removed from the church, but that left me free to seek. Praise God that the Word says, "seek and ye shall find" because I was more than ready to seek a better understanding.

Now, I certainly bear no ill feelings toward my former congregation, and I know many lovely people who love Jesus who attend denominational churches. In my case, though, the Pharisee Factor definitely played a major role in my inability to find joy, and then in my seeking a route that led me to joy. The lesson in my life is that you shouldn't let the Pharisee Factor be an excuse keeping you from your own relationship with God. Pharisees are not totally to blame for their behavior. They are human like all of us and they make mistakes. Before you write God off because of some human error, you should get to know him yourself and find out what you've been missing.

Never forget – and never let your children forget – that Jesus sent the Holy Spirit for each of us personally. He is not reserved for a chosen few. Jesus promises us in John 14 that He will reveal himself to us (personally and individually) and He will lead us and guide us in **all** truth. You should love your pastor, respect your pastor and listen to your pastor, and if he is a good pastor he will encourage you to seek God for yourself on your own.

You owe it to your children to get to know Jesus yourself. Don't you want to be the one to introduce them to Him? It was a tremendous benefit to my children that I found what I was seeking in Christ. Now, they know the Jesus I know, not the Pharisees I knew.

> *15 Woe unto you, scribes and Pharisees, hypocrites! For you compass the sea and land to make one proselyte and when he is made ye make him twofold more the child of hell than yourselves. (KJV)*

Even those of us who consider ourselves people of faith are guilty of this Pharisee Factor. When so many of us first become excited over our newfound walk with God, we naturally want to share it with others. Most of us still have so far to go, though, that we can do harm to innocent souls.

We Christians all know that we are commissioned to go into the entire world and share the gospel, right? The only problem with that is that we *have to know some of it in order to share it.* When I first became a Christian, I was so excited that I wanted to share all of my "wisdom" and "knowledge' with everyone who crossed my path. That's all good on paper, but when you take a newly-converted Christian with a lot of old religious baggage, it can cause a lot of trouble when you turn her loose on the unsaved.

While all of us have good intentions, we need to be careful that our zealousness for God doesn't become an oppressive weight of guilt and condemnation to our newfound disciples *and* to our children as we attempt to raise them. We need to be careful that we don't pressure people to do everything exactly as we do. Maybe those we lead into the kingdom aren't ready to hear how God speaks to us every day. Maybe their schedule doesn't allow them to get up early and pray two hours before work.

Maybe – contain your surprise – they don't *want* to pray two hours before work.

When we first become Christians, we are all infants and should be allowed to grow. We all start on milk before we progress to meat. And, just like infants, we all grow spiritually in different ways. That's the beauty of having a PERSONAL relationship with God. Not all of your children will grow at the same pace spiritually either.

God has a special and unique plan for every single person. In our children's lives, we are God's hands, but we are not God. We can lead our children with our words, our actions and the examples we set, but then we have to step aside and let God do His thing. As parents, we are not expected to have all of the answers for every question in a child's life. We should introduce them to God, teach them to seek God and pray for them. We can actually hurt a child's spiritual walk if we insist they do everything that *we* believe to be spiritual or if we compare them to other children who we believe have progressed farther in their spirituality.

Our fourth daughter has an incredible amount of faith and an incomprehensible amount of compassion toward others. Praying for others comes easily for her. She is selfless, loving, gentle and honest to the core. She will point out hypocrisy in others, but will do it with a smile on her face that will simply melt you.

Our oldest daughter, on the other hand, is much more practical than compassionate. Her prayers often revolve around plans and goals she has. While the two girls are totally different in their approach, neither is more spiritual. The Bible tells us that we are parts of one body. Maybe Michelle, our fourth daughter, is the body's heart, and her call may be to enter evangelism or missions. Colleen, our oldest daughter, may be the body's hand of leadership whose call may be to succeed financially. Someone has to finance the church.

We can't be quick to put our children into a box, just to make our own spiritual walk more comfortable. Many of us as parents will pray for things for our children that we think they need, or that we believe they should become. Our job is to pray for their protection from above, to be thankful for the health that Jesus purchased for them on the cross, and to turn them over to God to bring forth **His** will in their lives.

I have learned not to impose my will upon my children in my prayers. If you really want your children to be happy and to succeed, then get out of

God's way. Here is how I pray for my children:

> "Dear father, I thank you for the gift of these children that you have given to me. Please Father; give me the wisdom to raise them as you would have me. Correct me quickly and clearly if I am in your way. I turn them over to you completely and I rely on you to guide me where they are concerned. Reveal Yourself to me through your word so that I can reveal You to them, and give me the courage to stand firm when I need to stand firm. Show me how and when to be merciful. Please help me to be a doorway to You and not a roadblock. Thank you for your word. Thank you for your protection. Thank you that we are not of this world. Thank you for your favor. Thank you for your Son and our salvation. Thank you that you have a good plan for this family. Thank you that you promise to direct my steps if I put my trust in you. I thank you that you have equipped me for motherhood and I surrender myself to You and thank You for wisdom that You promised to give liberally. I pray that You would not allow me to misrepresent You to them. I want Your will in their lives. I pray that Your presence would follow them and that Your hand would be on them. I pray that You would protect their minds. I rebuke the

devourer in Jesus' name and I thank you that no weapon formed against them shall prosper. THANK YOU, THANK YOU, THANK YOU. You are an awesome God."

Some may believe it's a cop-out for parents to turn so much responsibility over to God. If you really have faith in God, though, it would be dangerous for you not to rely on Him completely. With all of the baggage that some of us bring into adulthood, we need to rely on God to raise our children. I have a tremendous desire – not a burden – to allow my children to find God. Because we are all still discovering our own relationship with our Heavenly Father, we can't allow our doubts or lack of wisdom to limit our children's relationship with Him.

If I had submitted to my parent's arm's-length relationship with God, I would have settled for the idea that I could not speak to God and would have been doomed to a life of cold, empty nothingness. My life would have borne no fruit and offered no joy. Then, I would have passed along that same mentality to my own children. Don't let the Pharisee Factor hold your children back from knowing God.

Parents should be doorways to God, not roadblocks. He will provide you with everything you need. Your job is to seek His face. Trust His word. Obey His spirit, and walk in His love. If your desire is to raise stable, powerful, content children, but the task seems too overwhelming, then you need to turn to Psalm 37:3-6:

*Trust (lean on, and be confident) in the Lord and do good so shall you dwell in the land and feed surely on His faithfulness, and truly shall you be fed. Delight yourself in the Lord and **he will give you the desires of your heart**. Commit your way to the Lord (roll and repose each care of your load on Him); trust (lean on, rely on, and be confident) also in him and **He will bring it to pass**. (Amplified)*

All families should take the time to look at the Pharisee Factor as well when it comes to their finances. Take a look at verse 16:

Woe to you blind guides, who say if anyone swears by the sanctuary of the temple, it is nothing; but if anyone swears by the gold of the sanctuary he is a debtor (bound by his oath. 17 You blind fools! For which is greater: the gold or the sanctuary of the temple that has made the gold sacred? 18 You say too, whoever swears by the altar is not duty bound but whoever swears by the offering on the alter s oath is binding. 19 You blind men, which is greater: the gift or the altar which makes the gift sacred?

There are Pharisees that put a lot of emphasis on money and offerings. While there is no doubt that tithes and offerings are an essential part of the

Christian walk, we shouldn't misunderstand how God feels about money. Your attitude toward money and God are vital in the spiritual and financial development of your children. The main thing God wants us to know is that we can never buy God's love or favor.

God does want to get involved in your finances, but, specifically, it's the spirit behind your giving that interest Him. Do your offerings come because you love and trust God, or do you give a particular amount so you can feel like you've done your duty to get on God's good side? Well, here's a bulletin. God doesn't need your money. Your money is a tool God has given you to increase *your* faith, not His. There's a great deal of understanding to be found on the issue of offerings in the story of the widow woman in the book of Mark:

> Mark 12:38-44 *38 And in (the course) of his teaching, he said, Beware of the scribes who like to go around in long robes and (to get) greetings in the marketplaces (public forums) 39 And have the front seats in the synagogues and the chief couches (place of honor) at feasts. 40 Who devour widows houses and to cover it up make long prayer. They will receive the heavier (sentence of) condemnation. 41 He sat down opposite the treasury and saw how the crowd was casting moneys into the treasury. Many rich were throwing in large sums. 42 And a widow who was poverty stricken has put in more than all those*

contributing to the treasury. 44 For they all threw in out of their abundance; but she out of her deep poverty has put in everything that she had (even) all she had on which to live.

Most people who are Pharisee-minded would say, God wants it all and He won't bless us if we don't give him everything we have. The Pharisees will tell you that giving those two mites was the only way for the widow woman to prove to God that she loved Him. And, they would say, because she couldn't give as much as others, she just had to hope that God would feel particularly generous that day and pull her through despite the paucity of her offering.

Jesus said Himself that he requires no other sacrifice other than the sacrifice of praise. He tried to tell his disciples that the widow had to have a tremendous amount of faith in God and His ability to provide her for *because* she gave all she had. You will notice that the story doesn't say that the widow woman gave her two mites and then turned around and told everyone about it. She made a huge sacrifice without telling anyone how hard it was.

God wants us to give in faith and with a cheerful and glad heart. He also says not to let the right hand know what the left has done. When you give, let it be between you and God. If you feel the urge to talk about your giving to others, then check the motive behind those desires? Are you sharing this information so that others will be encouraged to give also? Or are you sharing knowledge of your generosity so that people will admire what you have done?

If you are guilty of the latter, then you are stealing your own blessings. And, if you are providing this kind of example to your own children, then you are stealing their future blessings.

You don't want your children to see God as one who rewards only those who can give a lot to the cause. Don't ever fall for gimmicks that promise you special blessings if you give a certain dollar amount to a ministry. By doing this, you are participating in the very type of Pharisee Factor that holds thousands of good people back from giving, and understanding God's true intent when it comes to giving.

> *25 Woe to you scribes and Pharisees, pretenders, (Hypocrites) For you clean the outside of the cup and of the plate, but within they are full of extortion (prey spoil plunder) and grasping self-indulgence. 26 You blind Pharisees first clean the inside of the cup and of the plate so that the outside may be clean also. 27 Woe to you scribes and Pharisees pretenders (hypocrites)! For you are like tombs that have been whitewashed which look beautiful on the outside but inside are full of dead men's bones and everything impure. 28 Just so you also outwardly seem to people to be just and upright, but inside you are full of pretense and lawlessness and iniquity.*

In church people, you too often see behavior I call "spiritual status." That is when we do things as Christian parents because they look and sound good. For example, we hear parents boast, with a bit of a condescending tone, that they don't allow their children to watch television or listen to secular music. Yes, it is important to monitor what your children see and hear. But it is just as vital that we don't develop a false sense of success or status because we have a handle on a few physical behaviors, like watching television.

Shielding your children from bad influences **without** filling that time with something of value and providing them with examples of scriptural living will lead them just as far astray as a television show or popular music would. Be as concerned with their inner selves (their thoughts, their motives, and the condition of their hearts) as you are with their outside activities and you will see the fruits of your labor.

We owe it to our children and those who don't believe in our faith to *demonstrate the benefits of being a Christian.* Let them see us bear fruit from the way we live our lives, and then the activities of being a Christian will not be a heavy burden around their necks. Children are results-oriented. Not unlike us, they want to know, "What's in it for me?" How can they get a positive answer to that question if you can't show them what's happening in your own inner life?

You can be in church every single time the doors are open. You can sign your children up for every activity the church offers. But if you don't bear the fruit of righteousness, peace and joy, then you might just as well have stayed home and watched television. It is not enough to just hear the Word week after week. We have to show our children that the Word does work and that it is for our benefit. *Your children need to see that living a Godly life is one of privilege not prisoner.*

As a child, I remember wondering what was the point of our religious activities. We struggled to get to church, fought all the way home and endured the same old, same old all week long.

We should all compare our lives to the inside of a microwave oven.

One day, when I was cleaning up the kitchen after the kids left for school, the Lord gave me a revelation. I had done it all. I'd washed the dishes, swept the floor, wiped the counters and scrubbed the sink.

Then, I opened the microwave.

My initial reaction was just to throw the door shut again. This was much worse than any mess I'd seen lately. There was crusted chili dried on the oven's surface. Someone else had made oatmeal and the remains were hard as a rock on the microwave's turntable. To top it off, there was a layer of butter from some popcorn fixed the night before. I shut the door, looked at my otherwise clean kitchen, and told myself I could take care of the microwave later.

Then, the Lord spoke to my heart and said, "This is part of the problem a lot of Christians have. You do the exterior so that you look good. You show up, you smile and everything seems so perfect. You do the projects and you teach your children to master the behaviors of good little Christian children. But, on the inside, you are full of bitterness, jealousy, discontentment and hate. I am not nearly as impressed with your outward appearance as you think."

In my heart, God continued, "Get these things cleaned up, and then see what I will do. Don't put this task on the back burner."

The very best way for us to let God into our children's hearts is to let him into ours. He will get to them other ways, but why should we make them learn the hard way. So, I ask you, what does the inside of *your* microwave look like?

What we believe has a direct impact on our children. Getting to know the Father is far more important than the activities we do around the Father. Our children need to see Jesus **in** us. Jesus didn't run around in a panic all of the time, wondering if he was doing the right thing. He spent time with His Father and His Father ordered his steps. He came to be our example and to show us the direction in which to go.

Do we exhibit this knowledge, though, in the way in which we live? If you are a new Christian, congratulations, you'll get to know God with your children. If you have been a Christian for a while but would like a deeper walk with God, then all you have to do is take that first step. And if you are not a Christian, please don't hold us accountable for the mistakes of a few Pharisees.

Just as there are a few athletes who do drugs and rape women hasn't stopped me from enjoying sports. Likewise, a few misguided Pharisees shouldn't steal from you what God can provide. The Word is a lamp unto our feet so the path will be easy for all of us to follow. Just make sure you keep walking.

Don't limit God. Don't allow the Pharisee Factor to keep you from what God has for you and your family. Matthew 13:16-17 says:

> *16 But blessed (happy, fortunate and to be envied) are your eyes because they do see, and your ears because they do hear. 17 Truly I tell you, many prophets and righteous men (Men who were upright and in right standing with God) Yearn to see what you see, and did not see it, and to hear what you hear, and did not hear it. (Amplified)*

There are many well-meaning church-going believers, and even church leaders, who are longing for more than they are currently experiencing. There is only so much that religion can offer you. 2 Timothy 3:16-17 tells us that ALL scripture is inspired and given by God. It goes on to say that the scriptures are given for our benefit.

Take advantage of all that God has for you. Dare to believe it, and watch it work for your children.

CHAPTER EIGHT

Effective on the Battlefield

How victorious are you?
Interesting question, isn't it? As adults, we don't always think of our lives in terms of victories. But maybe we should. How victorious are you in your marriage, in your personal relationships, in your relationship with your children, in your parenting skills, in your finances, and even in your spiritual walk?

Do you find yourself feeling as if every area of your life is lacking something? Or, worse yet, are you someone who wakes up feeling as if your entire existence lacks quality?

I lived that way for a very long time. Seeing and cataloguing all of my shortcomings, I felt as if I would never arrive at the place in life I wanted to be. There seemed such a long way to go, and I feared I would never have enough days on earth to become the person I wished.

Although it happens on a completely different level, your children suffer from these same feelings. They frequently compare themselves to others. They begin to formulate plans for their lives. They experience success and failure just as we do. And they are definitely developing visions of the type of student, friend, athlete and even son or daughter they wish to be.

Your children experience the fear of having a chasm between who they are and who they aim to be. Keeping your eyes forward on the person you desire to be can be a healthy thing as long as you can keep the gap between your real and ideal selves in perspective.

Paul had these same issues in his life. He tells us in Romans 7:19:

> *19 For I fail to practice the good deeds I desire to do, but the evil deeds that I do not desire to do are what I am ever doing. 20 Now if I do what I do not desire to do, it is no longer I doing it (it is not myself that acts), but the sin (principle) which dwells within me fixed and operating in my soul. 21 So I find it to be a law (rule of action of my being) that when I want to do what is right and good evil is ever present with me and I am subject to its insistent demands. 22 For I endorse and delight in the Law of God in my inmost self (With new nature). 23 But I discern in my bodily members (in the sensitive appetites and wills of the*

flesh) a different law (rule of action) at war against the law of my mind (my reason) and making me a prisoner to the law of sin that swells in my bodily organs. (in the sensitive appetites and wills of the flesh) (Amplified)

We're constantly waging a battle, but it is not one of flesh and blood. The battle is of a spiritual nature. Because you are a spirit, you have the ability to fight the battle. Unfortunately, you are trapped in a body and you have a soul, which is your mind, your will and your emotions. Just as a battle between flesh and spirit wages within you, so it does within your children. Galatians 5:17 tells us:

For the flesh lusts against the Spirit and the Spirit against the flesh and these are contrary one to the other so that ye cannot do the things that ye would. (KJV)

We all know that the battle between flesh and spirit goes on everyday. It's a part of our daily experiences. I wonder, though, if we all understand that we have been supplied with everything we need to be victorious in this battle. It's essential that we do, because teaching our children to be warriors and to be effective on the battlefield is vital to their success as a person, to the development of their Spirit, and to the taming of their soul.

According to the Word, God tells us that we are always triumphant and always victorious

(2 Corinthians 2:14). We can hear and read these words. We can say that we believe them. But, do we live as if we are victorious? In order for us to teach our children how to become effective in battle, we need to understand a few principles about how this war is to be fought. Again, the very best way to teach a child how to be an effective warrior is to become one yourself.

How do you become an effective warrior? The first step is to recognize your enemy and to understand his tactics. For a long time, Christians have been trying to fight the devil. Many of us fight him on his terms, in his territory and by his rules. We do this because we have a poor understanding of who the devil really is and what weapons he uses against us.

According to Hollywood, the devil is either a fire breathing dragon or a malignant force that makes our heads spin 360 degrees and forces us to expel split pea soup in all directions. Those are movie fantasies, but the fact of the matter is, that there is indeed a devil and he is our enemy. The Word tells us "we wrestle not with flesh and blood, but with powers and principalities, and rulers of the dark places and against spiritual wickedness in high places." (Ephesians 6:12)

Once you understand who the devil is and how he functions, you will be able to fight him in the manner that God intended. The result will be more triumph than tragedy in your life.

The Enemy

In the book of Isaiah, we learn where the devil

himself originated. Lucifer was one of God's most glorious heavenly creatures. He was adorned with instruments made of fine gold and precious jewels. He was in close relationship with God and had a special place in the heavenly realm. Unfortunately, Lucifer was afflicted with pride. When he exalted himself against God, he gave up his place in heaven and was cast down to earth.

> Isaiah 14:10-12 *All men will tauntingly say to you, have you also become weak as we are? Have you become like us? Your pomp and magnificence are brought down to Sheol (the underworld) along with the sound of your harps; the maggots (which prey upon dead bodies) are spread out under you and worms cover you. 12 How have you fallen from heaven O light bringer and daystar son of the morning? How you have been cut down to the ground you who weakened and laid low the nations.*

> Verse 16 *Those who see you will gaze at you and say, "Is **this** the man who made the earth tremble? Who shook the kingdoms? (Amplified)*

I believe these verses are talking about our future, and a future even beyond our lives. Isaiah is making the point that all of us will someday be able to see Satan for what he really is. If we've grown to a mature spiritual level, we will see him as nothing more than a worm-covered defeated foe. OR, if we haven't matured spiritually, we'll look at Satan one day and say incredulously, **that** is what I let stand between my life and everything I could have accomplished?

> John 8:44 *When he speaks a falsehood he speaks what is natural to him. For he is a liar and the father of lies and of all that is false. (KJV)*

> I Peter 5:8 *For the enemy of yours the devil, roams around like a roaring lion seeking whom he may devour. (Amplified)*

> Romans 16:20 *And the God of peace shall bruise Satan under your feet shortly. The grace of our Lord Jesus Christ be with you. (KJV)*

> Acts 2:35 *Until I make your enemies a footstool for your feet.*

> Colossians 2:15 *And having spoiled principalities and powers, He made a show of them openly, triumphing over them. (KJV)*

From these scriptures, we can see that Satan is a liar and the father of anything that is false. He is in disguise to resemble a lion, but he isn't one. He is obviously bruised and under our feet. And, when

Jesus descended into hell for three days after his crucifixion, he stripped Satan and all principalities of their authority and powers leaving them humiliated and defeated.

Does this really sound to you like a tough enemy?

The problem we face is not Satan, this defeated foe, himself, but rather the weapons he uses. Satan knows his place. He knows he is powerless, defeated and that his days are numbered. But he is also the king of deception and has played a sinister trick on most people. He makes *us* our own worst enemies.

Remember that battle we've talked about – flesh versus spirit? It's *our* flesh against *our* spirit. The Amplified Bible describes Satan as the "enemy of your soul." Your soul is your mind, your will and your emotions. This is the battlefield on which you and your children are forced to fight.

But, we're created to fight this battle. Ephesians Chapter 6 tells us that we have at our disposal the breastplate of righteousness, the shield of faith, the helmet of salvation, the sword of the spirit (the word of God), the belt of truth and the shoes of peace. There is no denying that Christians have the proper armor to be victorious.

If we are so well equipped, then why are so many of our Christian friends in debt, getting divorced, miserably depressed or addicted to drugs or alcohol? This shouldn't be the case if our enemy is already defeated.

The problem is that many of us are trying to fight naked. I can testify that, for years, I was running around without my armor on. I could quote the scripture, but I didn't take the lessons to heart in terms of arming myself for the battles we all face.

Let's look at it this way. Say you joined the military and you were preparing to head into your first major conflict. Your commanding officer hands you your gear. "Ok, son, now here is your helmet to protect your head, your gun and ammunition belt, and your boots for the rough terrain we're going to encounter. Make sure you have your bulletproof vest, and your mission manual with all of our coordinates so that you can find your way back to camp if you get off course." You respond with a confident, "Yes, sir!"

Then, the next day, you show up in your underwear.

Many of you are, figuratively speaking, sitting in your underwear right now. I ran around trying to fight the devil this way for a long time, not using the armor provided to me. Let me tell you, it's hard work to fight that way, and more than a little humiliating. Ephesians 6:13 tells us that God provides the armor we need, but that it takes a step of faith and obedience to **put it on**.

One of the strongest weapons Satan uses against all people is the weapon of suggestion. All day long, our mind is filled with thoughts both good and bad. Have you ever noticed that it is possible to get caught up in these thoughts to a degree that you can't even believe it's you thinking about them? This is how Satan attacks your mind. Remember, he is the father of lies, so you can bet most of the things he tells you are not true.

Satan's suggestions can lead to some of the greatest casualties of war. His suggestions enter through your mind and then tie up your emotions. Pretty soon, you can even feel your internal organs responding to these thoughts. Whether they are thoughts of fear, pride, anger or depression, you feel your heart pound, your countenance change, and perhaps even tears upon your cheeks. This emotional upheaval happens when your enemy makes a mere suggestion, and you in your nakedness do not have the wherewithal to fend it off.

Sooner or later, your behavior will be affected. You may yell at your children, accuse your husband, destroy friendships, and possibly even hurt yourself — all because you don't have the armor on to protect yourself against negative thoughts.

These scenarios have played themselves out dozens of times in your life, but you need to realize that your children go through the same kind of turmoil. Have any of your children ever come to you after a hard day at school and said, "I don't think very many people like me," or "I think I am fat and ugly," or "my teacher hates me." As a parent, you have a couple of options in these situations. You can, as I like to say, pooh-pooh the issue by telling your children that everything will be better tomorrow. Or, you can address these issues and talk meaningfully to your children about them.

All of these types of statements originate in the *minds* of your children. When you avoid addressing your children's turmoil, you leave the door wide open for the devil to raise havoc in their minds.

God has given you and your family everything you need to address anything that the devil can throw at you. Whether it is thoughts of fear, dread, worry, depression, insufficiency, rage, sickness or even self-pity, you have what you need to combat it.

But you also have a responsibility to do something.

Too many Christians live their lives thinking God is going to take care of everything. Yes, God is in control, but he has equipped us to live a life of victory. It is our choice whether to live that kind of life. By believing God's word and choosing to fight this battle, we prove our faith in God and in His word. If, however, we leave everything up to chance, then we let the devil run wild in our thoughts. And, worse yet, we miss the opportunity to teach our children the importance of waging battle.

If you don't choose to prepare for the fight, you may tell everyone that you are a Christian but you will live with all of the same emotional problems as those who are not. You will not be triumphant or victorious, nor will you be a good witness. It's not that you're a bad person, or that God loves you any less.

It's just that....well, you're running around in your underwear.

So, what are our options in dealing with troublesome thoughts? In the following scriptures, we see that we have a few tactics to help use against those fiery darts the devil puts into our minds. Our first task is to process whether a thought comes from God or not. If it is not uplifting, edifying, or convincing us to change for the better, then we can assume the thought is belittling, condemning or anxious and must thus be addressed. Once the thought enters our mind, we must choose to change it or reject it.

> Proverbs 23:7 *As a man thinketh in his heart so is he. (KJV)*

> Psalm 94:19 *In the multitude of my (anxious) thoughts within me, Your comforts cheer and delight my soul. (Amplified)*

> Proverbs 16:3 *Roll your works upon the Lord (commit, and trust them wholly to him; He will cause your thoughts to become agreeable to His will and) so shall your plans be established and succeed. (Amplified)*

> Philippians 4:8 *Finally brethren whatsoever things are true, whatsoever things are honest, whatsoever things are just, whatsoever things are pure, whatsoever things are lovely, whatsoever things are of good report, if there be any virtue and if there be any praise think on these things. (KJV)*

> 2 Corinthians 10:5 *Casting down imaginations and every high thing that exalts itself against the knowledge of God and bringing*

into captivity every thought to the obedience of Christ. (KJV)

These scriptures tell us that we have the ability to change the thoughts that enter our minds. We need to know God's Word so that we can be comforted. We need to give up our thoughts and commit to the ways of God because he will make our thoughts His thoughts if we are willing to submit them to him.

Part of putting on our armor has to do with taking control of our thoughts and refusing to dwell on those which are not of God. We need to fill our minds with what God says about us, to us, and for us in his Word.

Hebrews 4:11 *For the Word that God speaks is alive and full of power, (making it active, energizing, and effective). It is sharper than any two-edged sword penetrating to the dividing line of the breath of life (soul) and the (immortal) spirit and of joint and marrow (of the deepest parts of our nature)* **exposing and sifting and analyzing and judging the very thoughts and purposes of the heart.** *(Amplified)*

Paul is trying to make the point that God already knows what we need, and is ready and willing to give it to us if we will have faith instead of fear, belief instead of doubt, and trust instead of anxiety. Satan wants to kill your joy, steal your faith and destroy your life by dominating your thoughts. The way you allow him to do that is to take the thoughts that he puts into your mind.

We know that God has not given us a spirit of fear, but rather of peace, love and a sound mind. (2 Timothy 1:7) So, the next time you begin entertaining thoughts that you know did not come from God, you have an option. Change your mind. This will be hard at first, but God will honor your step of faith. Don't be surprised, though, if the devil puts pressure on you. Just remember to stand your ground, submit to God's way of thinking, and the devil will have no choice but to flee.

Listen to your children. Watch your children. Their thoughts will be revealed to you in their words and in their actions. Take the time to notice the changes in their countenance and mood. Because they are young, they don't know where their thoughts originate, so you need to show them.

Children love to be victorious. One day, Michelle was walking through the house and I heard her say, "I hope I don't get the flu, I *think* I'm getting a headache." I didn't say a thing. I just looked at her and, before I could even speak, she smiled at me and said, "What I meant to say was, get back under my feet where you belong, devil."

You must teach your children to stand their ground and change their thoughts by applying the Word. How different would our world be if more parents took the time to ask their children what they are thinking about?

Trust me, I have read through to the end of the

Book, and the good guys win. Put on your armor and keep standing.

CHAPTER NINE

The Power of Choice

One of my absolute, positively favorite scripture versus comes from Deuteronomy 30:19:

I call heaven and earth to witness this day against you that I have set before you life and death, the blessings and the curses; therefore choose life that you and your descendants may live. (Amplified)

God gave all of us the most powerful tool we can possibly possess in this world. Not only did he give it to us, but he told us what would happen if we learned how to use it.

That tool is choice.

It's amazing that God bestowed us with this tool. He could have literally made us perfect creatures that would do everything right all of the time. Instead, He proved His love by giving us the right to choose. One of the greatest disservices we can do to our children is to not inform them of their power of choice. Since God allowed us to choose, it is essential that we follow His example and teach our children the impact of making choices. I read and had a good understanding of this scripture when I was young in my Christian walk. It has been invaluable to me in *preparing* my children for life.

Discipline has everything to do with teaching your children how powerful their choices are. When our children were very small, it would have been easy to get caught in a trap of chasing them around the house saying "no, no" all of the time. Instead, I would say things like, "You need to stop jumping on the couch. If you do not stop jumping, mommy is going to spank you. The choice is yours, do you want to stop or do you want a spanking?"

Obedience will tell them to stop jumping. Their flesh will tell them, "come on, mom, and show me what you're made of." Of course, our children are not always going to make the right choice – even when the options are so clear. The importance here is that they understand that the outcome is in their hands.

I believe I was fortunate to have my children at a very young age. Not many of my friends could give me parenting advice, because they had not yet had children. Today, a lot of my friends have small children or babies, and it is so much fun to watch them try all of the techniques they pick up from books and magazines. Every parent wants to do what is best for his or her child. Yet, so many of them miss a fundamental truth about parenting. *The greatest gift you can give your child is the ability to make well-thought out choices.*

And, the best way to teach your children how to make quality choices is to let them choose. There's a fine line to walk here. Some parents let the power of choice get out of hand, by allowing their children either too many choices or asking them to make choices they're not yet ready to handle. Children are not mentally mature enough to make choices about what preschool they should attend, what time is appropriate for bedtime, whether mommy should have another baby, or who should be in charge at home. On the other hand, children are well-equipped to make choices about obedience.

In Deuteronomy, God says very clearly, "If you adhere to my commandment, you will be blessed. If you do not, you will be cursed." He makes this abundantly clear. Yet, even as adults, we still feel the need to test Him at times to see if he really means it. Your children will test you in the same way to see if you mean what you say. It's vital that parents be like God and mean it. You must be consistent and relentless when it comes to proving to your children that choice is powerful, and that the outcome of choice is theirs. If you teach this to your children when they are young, not only will you exemplify God, but your children will learn to trust you and to trust God.

The issue here is not spanking. Spanking just happened to work really well for me, but that's a parental choice. What is most important is that you mean what you say, and say what you mean, and that you carry out your words.

If you teach your children that choices have consequences, and that they will be held accountable for the choices that they make, they will be less likely to fall into temptation when they are teens and young adults. They will not see temptation as an irresistible force, but rather they will see it as a matter of serious consideration and contemplation. When children are small, they are at their most impressionable. This is when you must, as a parent, consistently show your child that good choices result in blessing and bad choices result in cursing. Then, as they get older, these teachings will be ingrained in them and they will be less likely to push them aside in the heat of the moment. They **will** think before they act.

Choices children make at a young age may seem insignificant. For example, your four-year-old may need to choose between eating his carrots and being able to play outside, or passing on the carrots and having to stay in his room. This may seem like a petty matter for an adult but, to a four-year-old, going outside to play is like winning the lottery. Too many parents miss these opportunities to teach their children valuable lessons about choice. They may think they don't have enough energy to follow through on the choices they offer their children. When the child has a tantrum about eating the carrots, a tired parent may just throw their hands up in surrender and say, "fine, just go outside."

What they have done in that case is given the child a blessing for making the wrong choice. This, I

To Prepare or To Protect

believe, is the primary reason we see so much disobedience and lack of respect in young people today. Children who aren't made to see the consequence of bad choices lose faith in their parent's ability to prepare them and care for them. They become confused and eventually treat all authority – teachers, coaches, and law enforcement – with the same disregard they show their parents.

Don't ever become so weary with the day-to-day grind of life that you stop proving to your children that their choices are important. I can sympathize with frazzled mothers. Remember, I had five children who were under the age of seven. And, if you have a strong-willed child, it's definitely a drain on your energies. But, if you don't understand the principle of choice, then you will be frazzled for years and years, instead of for just the few years when your children are very young.

Once your children believe that you will follow through on the choices you give them, and once they understand that bad choices produce bad results, they will start to make good choices on a regular basis. Actually, children catch onto this concept much faster than many adults. I know people in their 30's who still believe that the good and bad circumstances in their lives just come their way as a matter of luck and happenstance.

As your children enter their teenage years, the choices they face are going to get tougher. It is critical that you been consistent in your teaching about choices, and that you have followed up on your words. Now, what if your child was faced with the choice of trying drugs or alcohol at a party? Nearly every parent in America has had a talk with their children about the dangers of using drugs or alcohol. But, when faced with this choice, if your child feels that you don't often mean what you say and say what you mean, then it will be much easier for him to give into temptation.

You – and your son or daughter – will be reaping the curse of not holding that child accountable time after time for the little choices he made as a small child.

I have three teenage daughters, all of whom are starting to go out more and do more with their friends. I believe with all my heart that my girls understand the power of choice. Do they always make the right choices? Being human, they probably don't every single time. They do, however, make more right choices than wrong ones. They know that their parents have spend endless hours talking with them about how hard life can be. We share with them the wrong choices we made as teenagers and how those choices affected our lives. We also share with them our right choices, ones that were sometimes hard to make and stick with.

Children want to know that their parents understand how they feel and what they are experiencing. They need to know that their parents are strong enough to help them when the time comes to face tough situations. While you may not be physically standing with them when tough choices are before them, your voice will be inside their heads at those critical times – *if* you have been consistent in your

To Prepare or To Protect

teachings.

There will come times in your children's lives when they will either wish you were tougher, or they will thank God that you were tough. You have the ability to help your children avoid the type of mistakes that can change their lives forever. It starts when they are toddlers.

Our children know the impact of their choices, and have sometimes found out the hard way. My oldest daughter, Colleen, is a great kid, but extremely strong-willed – like her mother. We've spent much time working on her self-control when it came to handling her temper and arguing with us. One night, she wanted to go somewhere that her father and I didn't think she needed to be. She ranted and raved, giving every reason why we were the most unfair parents in the world. Colleen told us that we had no idea how awful it was to have to live with us. It was, in other words, pretty normal teenage stuff.

As I've noted earlier, my husband is not one to participate in a shouting match, and he's not much for debating either. He told her calmly, "I have decided that you have crossed the line here and you are not going out tonight. This can be the end of the argument right now or you can continue to try to prove your point. I am telling you, though, that if you open your mouth and raise your voice to me, you are going to be grounded for three weeks."

That wasn't going to stop Colleen. He had barely finished the sentence when she was responding with her next reason for wanting to go out that night. He smiled at her and said, "You are grounded. Please go to your room." At that moment, she remembered that her best friend's 16th birthday party was taking place in three days. This party had been in the works for months, and Colleen had been intensely looking forward to it. Her demeanor changed and she said, "Daddy, you don't mean that I can't go to Sara's birthday, right?"

He said again, "You are grounded for three weeks. You cannot go anywhere."

At this point, even I was in shock. I'm sure my job dropped because I knew how much Colleen had talked about this party and how much it meant to her. Colleen was really mad now and she let her dad have it with both barrels. He sat and listened to her for a while and then, in all his wisdom, he said, "I don't know why you are so mad at me. I gave you the opportunity to choose. I could have just grounded you for your behavior before this. It is not my fault that you are not going to the party. It was your choice."

After he said that, she had no response. Based on past experience she knew he meant what he said, and she knew that she had made the wrong choice.

She did ask me to intervene on her behalf, and I did talk to him. What he said to me made a huge impact on me. He said, "We have worked too hard for too long to teach her the power of her choices. If we give in to this, it will be a turning point in her life and we will have failed. We have four more daughters to go and we must stay steady. If we give in now, this will continue until she leaves this house. If you stick with me on this, she will learn exactly what we have always tried to teach her. But if you cave in, we are going to have to put up with this every time she wants to do something that we don't want her to do."

Sometimes it's hard for parents to stick to a plan. In this case, though, my husband was definitely right. I stuck with him and told her that there was nothing she could do to change our minds. As a mother, I could soften the blow a little bit by explaining to her that everything we do is because we love her. And I stressed that, while she may not understand or agree with us, that she must still obey and respect us. I also told her that I felt very badly that she could not go to the party, and that I knew it must have been very difficult for her to call her friends to tell them she wouldn't be there. I told her that I would take her to buy a gift that she could send with someone else. When we talked, she told me, "I know it is my fault that I can't go and I am sorry that I said I hated you. *I really thought that you guys would give in this time.*"

Your children will go through these same struggles. Life is hard for kids, but it will be much harder if you don't teach them the power of their choices. We've never had another incident like that one with Colleen since. She has disagreed with us, but she has always chosen not to fight. She has never been late for her curfew, and she has made excellent choices when it comes to selecting friends. She's simply a great person to be around. But, I wonder how differently things would be if we had given in? I wonder how many battles we would have had to fight with her.

In the case of the birthday party, one wrong

choice on our part would have changed everything. If we had given in, we would have lost credibility in her eyes and we would have spent the next three years battling every decision. When you, as a parent, are faced with the choice to stay steady or to cave in with emotion, it is critical that you stay the course. What seems hard at that moment will bring you joy for a lifetime.

If you haven't been consistent up to now, don't feel as if it is a lost cause. Children love their parents. All you have to do is go to your child, humble yourself and apologize, and let them know that things will be changing. Make sure you point out when you are disciplining a bad choice or rewarding a good one. It won't take long before they catch on to your new, and better, policy.

We must teach our children to weigh the choices they make. The ability to choose to be peaceful is not enough if your child doesn't understand the benefits that come with that choice. Avoiding drugs is a good choice, but young people must see that there is a reward that goes with that choice. That is what "weighing" your choice means. They must have the reinforcement and past experience that their good choices have been rewarded and their bad choices have been disciplined.

In the area of discipline, many parents tend to focus only on the bad choices our children make. We somehow assume that it is easier to teach a lesson when something bad has happened. This may stem from the way we were raised or just how society as a whole responds to bad choices. In the experiences I have had with parents, it seems to me there is generally a direct correlation between how a parent disciplines and what their perception of God is.

In my own upbringing, my dad's perception of God was and still is one of a God who is simply waiting for us to make mistakes so He can punish us. In his view, the purpose of God is not to show us love, but rather to "stick it to us" when we make a mistake. As a child, this was very hard because someone was always waiting for you to make a mistake so that they could point it out and punish you for it.

This does not lead to a productive parent-child relationship. The child will eventually feel that, no matter what he does or how hard he tries, he can't be perfect and avoid mistakes. And if you can't be perfect, then what's the use in trying. Children in this kind of upbringing go in one of two directions. Either they become very rebellious and engage in bad behavior, believing it won't matter anyway, or they become very introverted and live lives of quiet desperation and guilt.

There's another extreme, seen in those people who excuse all behaviors to God's grace. Children raised by parents with this philosophy have problems of accountability. If you believe that God does not care what you do as long as you say you're sorry, then how can you ever hold your children accountable for their actions?

There is a fine line between these two extremes. It is very true that God does expect obedience from us and he does spell it out very clearly in His Word that there are blessings and curses based on the choices we make. It is also true that we are saved by grace and that God is loving and quick to forgive.

We must understand that we, like our children, are still growing. The measure of thought and study we give to the Word is the measure of accountability that we have to God. If your child never matured past the two-year-old level, that child's ability to make choices would be limited. And your ability as a parent to reward and punish would also be limited. The same is true with our relationship with God. If it never matures past the point of simply believing He exists, we limit God in the way he can bless and correct us. As Proverbs 3:12 says, *For whom the Lord loves He corrects even as a father corrects the son in whom he delights.*

If we want to successfully teach our children the power of choice, correction is a good thing when done appropriately. A vital part of correction is recognizing and rewarding good choices. If God does it for us, then we should learn from that and do it for our children.

> Deuteronomy 28: *If you will listen diligently to the voice of the Lord your God being watchful to do all His commandments which I command you this day, the Lord your God will set you high above all nations of the earth. 2 and all these blessings shall come upon you and overtake you if you heed the voice of the Lord your God. 3 Blessed shall you be in the city and*

To Prepare or To Protect

blessed shall you be in the field. 4 Blessed shall be the fruit of your body (your children) and the fruit of your ground and the fruit of your heards, the increase of your cattle and the young of your flock (Your job or your business). 5 Blessed shall be your baskets and your kneading troughs. 6 Blessed shall you be coming in and blessed shall you be going out. 7 The Lord shall cause your enemies who rise up against you to be defeated before your face; they shall come out against you one way and flee before you seven ways. 8 The Lord shall command the blessing upon you in your storehouse (saving and stock accounts) and in all that you undertake. And He will bless you in the land which the Lord your God gives you. 9 The Lord will establish you as a people holy to Himself as He has sworn to you, if you keep the commandment of the Lord your God and walk in His ways. 10 And all people of the earth shall see that you are called by the name and the presence of the Lord and they shall be afraid of you. ***11 And the Lord shall make you have a surplus of prosperity, through the fruit of your body, (your children) of your livestock, (your job or business) and of the ground, which the Lord swore to your fathers to give you. 12 The Lord shall open to you his good treasury, the heaven*** *to give the rain of your land in its season and to bless all the work of your hands and you shall lend to many nations but you shall not borrow. 13 And the Lord shall make you the head and not the tail and you shall be above only and you shall not be beneath if you heed the commandments of the Lord your God which I command you this day and are watchful to do them. (Amplified.)*

God spells out pretty clearly how we are able to live – that's *able* to live, not supposed to live, must live, or are forced to live. We acquire blessings if we make the right choices. On the flip side, God tells us in Deuteronomy 28 the consequences of making poor choices.

15 But if you will not obey the voice of the Lord your God being watchful to do all His commandments and his statutes, which I command you, this day then all these curses shall come upon you and overtake you. 16 Cursed shall you be in the city and cursed shall you be in the field. 17 Cursed shall be your basket and your kneading trough. 18 Cursed shall be the fruit of your body of your land of the increase of your cattle and the young of your sheep. 19 Cursed shall you be when you come in and cursed shall you be when you come out. 20 The Lord shall send you curses confusion and rebuke in every enterprise to which you sent your hand until you are destroyed perishing quickly because of the evil of your doing by which you have forsaken me. (Amplified)

In the next chapters of Deuteronomy, God continues to stress the blessing and the cursing. He goes into detail as to what His desires are and He even tells us how to repent if we slip up and make a bad choice. Then He sums it all up in Deuteronomy 30 when he gives us the choice and recommends his answer:

I call Heaven and earth to witness this day against you that I have set before you life and the blessings and death and the curses; therefore choose life that you and your descendants may live.

How cool is God? Not only does He spell out our choices in way that leave no doubt He means business, but he also gives us the right answer. Choose life. It is so simple, and yet we complicate His message so much. It would be like someone saying to you, "Here is a stack of hundred dollar bills, and here is a pile of cow manure. You choose which you would like to take home." Too many people would actually take the time to contemplate the choice because past influences have told them that nothing that good can come easily. Don't let past influences cloud your vision. Simply choose life.

Ask yourself an important question. If God is willing to do this for me, shouldn't I be willing to do the same for my children? All too many parents use phrases like, "because I said so", or "you'd better not every let me catch you..." or "do as I say, not as I do." Do yourself and your children a favor and give them something to think about, rather than just simple dictates. Every parent has apprehension about the issues we have to discuss with our children – sex, drugs, alcohol, lifestyles and friends. We need to make our children think about their choices so that they know what's at stake. God uses the phrase "if you" consistently throughout Deuteronomy, and I'm sure He wouldn't mind if you borrow it in your talks with your children.

One day, I saw Colleen drive off without her seat belt on. When she came home, I simply said to her, "*If you* drive without your seatbelt again, I will take your keys away for two weeks." Now, I am sure that every time she gets in her car she will think about that. If she forgets and, consequently, can't drive for two weeks, then I am positive she won't forget again.

Also, never forget to recognize your children's good choices. Nothing motivates a child more than to hear their parent say they are proud of them. Teenagers love to hear that they are mature. So, if your teen makes a mature choice, take note of it. I love to brag about my daughters to other people and, occasionally, I do it when they are there to hear. It's a reward for making good choices.

Bless them with material things at times too. We bought our oldest daughter a nice car when she got

To Prepare or To Protect

her driver's license, and we told her that the reason she got her own car was because she has made some great choices, when faced with tough circumstances. We also told her that we hope she continues to make good choices because a car carries with it a lot of expenses. These expenses could either be areas for us to bless her, or they may become curses to her, based on the choices she makes with the car. I guarantee she understands exactly what we mean.

Your children will not be children forever. You will not always be there to take care of the outcome of every one of their bad choices. The brunt of your job is over when your children realize the power of their choices. Everything you teach them today is the foundation for the rest of their lives. I always chuckle when people say they are "raising children." In actuality, we *have* children who we are raising into adults.

Part of our problem in this country is that people have decided you are not an adult until you turn 18 and, thus, you are not accountable for your actions until then. I have a 10-year-old child who is more mature than a lot of 18-year-old so-called adults. Your children do not magically become adults when they turn 18 or 21 or 25. A chronological age does not prepare them for life. It is the foundation that you provide for them that will determine the outcome of their life and their preparation for what comes.

I will never forget a conversation I had with a woman who was very bothered with me because I gave my children chores to do, and I would not let them play with her children until their chores were done. She told me I was only hurting them because life was going to be hard enough when they grew up and *had* to work. She said I should let them be children, and allow them to laugh and play and enjoy life. I explained to her that the reason I gave my children chores now is because I know that life will be hard. I want them to be able to laugh, play and enjoy their lives *then*. It is the foundation that *you* build that will determine the stability of the house that *they* live in.

> Matthew 7:24-27 *So everyone who hears these words of Mine and acts upon them (obeying them) will be like a sensible (prudent, practical, and wise) man who built his house upon the rock. And the rain fell and the floods came and the winds blew and beat against that house; yet it did not fall because it had been founded on the rock. And everyone who hears these words of Mine and does **not** do them will be like a stupid (foolish) man who built his house upon the sand. And the rains fell and the floods came and the winds blew and beat upon the house and it fell, **and great and complete was the fall of it**. (Amplified)*

Mistakes are inevitable. Even children who grow up in the most spiritual of homes with pastors as parents make bad choices sometimes. We all do. But if the foundation is laid correctly, they will recover from the outcome of those choices. Jesus tells us that the rain **will** come, and the wind **will** blow, and it **will** beat upon the house. It's not if, but when. Life **is** going to try to test your children. Your children may venture off track and they may experience some storm damage from life. If the foundation is strong, though, they will be too.

Your success as a parent is not based on the mistakes your children make. It is based on how they handle those mistakes once they make them.

God has been very faithful in blessing our family. I believe it is because of the choices we make. What better way to be an ambassador of God than to empower our children with the same ability to choose as He has given my husband and I? Don't grow old regretting that you did not teach your children the power of choice. Start today. Start assessing your own choices and you will be blessed in the city, blessed in the field, blessed coming in and blessed going out.

And the fruit of your body **will be blessed**.

CHAPTER TEN

Creating a Sanctuary

What is a sanctuary and why is it so important? A sanctuary according to Strong's Concordance is: *A place set aside, sacred, a place of immunity, safe from outside danger, a safe haven, and a consecrated place.* A sanctuary is vital because, without one, your child will be continuously at the mercy of an onslaught from the enemy. A sanctuary is a place where your child is safe from the jeers of their peers, and from the pressures of everyday life. It's a place where they can let their hair down and just be themselves. A sanctuary allows them the opportunity to blow off some steam when necessary. The very best place for your child to find their sanctuary is in their home.

In the past few years, unfortunately, the American household has resembled Grand Central Station more than it has a home. In many cases, children are only home long enough for sleep and a few quick meals. If that's the case, in your home, you are not providing them a basic necessity vital to survival in this world.

There is no shortage of little plaques and knick knacks that have the statement enscripted on them that says:

A house is made of sticks and stones a home is made of love alone.

Throughout this book I have tried to share that we are to be an example of God's nature to our children. Because God is love to us and He is our sanctuary, [Isa 8:14 *And He shall be a sanctuary, a sacred and indestructible asylum to those who reverently fear and trust in Him. (Amplified)*] We owe it to our children to provide them with the closest thing in our human ability that we can to God's sanctuary. 1 Corinthians chapter 13 describes to us what the God kind of love is. It is; patient, kind, it is never envious or boils over with jealousy. Love is not boastful, or vainglorious, it is not haughty. It is not conceited or arrogant and inflated with pride, it is not rude and unmannerly, love does not act unbecomingly. Love doesn't always insist on its own way, because it is not self-seeking. Love is not touchy or fretful. Love does not keep track of evil done and pays no attention to an offense. Love does not rejoice in injustice and unrighteousness, but it does rejoice when right prevails. Love bears up under anything and everything that comes, love always believes the best of every person. Love provides hope that is endless under all circumstances and it endures everything without weakening. Love

To Prepare or To Protect

never fails, or comes to an end.

When you think about all that your children endure in a day, you can see why they need a place of sanctuary. Only **you** can love your child with the kind of love that is necessary to promote this type of environment. You are the only one who knows and cares for them deeply enough and has enough at stake to provide that 1Corinthians chapter 13 kind of love.

Have you ever noticed that when a child or teenager has a really bad experience either at school or at a friend's house, the first thing they generally say is, "I just want to go home."? I remember once when I was very young, probably eight years old or so, my cousin and I were riding bikes. We were heading down this very steep hill. As our speed increased, the distance between our two bikes decreased. Suddenly, our spokes caught together. We plummeted down the hill in a careen of tires, handlebars, arms and legs.

We were both in pretty tough shape, bleeding from almost every extremity, and crying. In a few minutes, a man ran out to help me up and all I could say was, "I want to go home, please leave me alone, I just want to go home." Our bodies ached, our bikes were bent, yet my cousin and I pushed them home because that was the only place I knew that everything would be okay.

Even in the television sit-coms of my childhood, wives always threatened to go home to their mothers when things weren't going well. While I don't advocate running home to your mother when you are an adult, it's definitely true that there are still times even as adults that we long for that safe, protective feeling of being home.

Even more than when I was young, children today have a strong need for a place of sanctuary. They need a place where they feel safe, where they don't feel judged, where they don't have to put on a mask.

You can imagine that, with a household full of daughters, we have quite a few emotions flying around most of the time. Generally, every 25-30 days things get pretty far out there and nerves can get on edge. We have a rule at our house. That rule is that we are a family and we will do everything in our power to be kind and compassionate to each other. Yet, in the event of a hormonal meltdown we will be forgiving, patient, and kind to one another. Girls in general will say things to each other that can be hurtful. It's just a part of the emotional makeup God gave them. While I encourage anger management and self-control, I also understand that sometimes you just "gotta let it fly". It helps to have family members who will look past those overly emotional moments and focus on your good qualities, someone who will see the best in you even when you are at your worst.

Children have a lot of pressures put on them to be good at so many things, to be well behaved, to be good friends, athletes, students and good people. They need a place where there is an atmosphere of unconditional love to which they can go. Home is invaluable, if for nothing more than a hug and a cheerful, "How was your day?" Your home should be a place that generates feelings of peace and love, and enables children to breathe a sigh of relief that they made it there and can recuperate for another day. It should not be a place of chaos, commotion, and strife.

Because peace is a major priority in our family, people who visit us will make comments like, "there is just something about your house, I can't put my finger on it but I like it." All of our girls have friends that will come over and say, "I just love it here I could stay here forever."

That brings up an important point. As I have mentioned, I believe that **all** children need a sanctuary. If it is not their own homes, they will find sanctuary somewhere. Every child needs a place where they are accepted, where they can feel a part of something bigger than themselves. For children who can't find a safe home as sanctuary, gangs become an unhealthy refuge where they can find some form of acceptance.

We should make an effort to provide sanctuary to those children who don't have a home that serves as a safe haven. You may need to be the provider of a sanctuary for those children who do not have a healthy environment of their own. I would encourage you to look at this as an opportunity and not a burden. You very well could be the person or family that could make all the difference in another child's life.

What can you do to create a sanctuary for your children? We covered how important peace is and that it needs to be a priority in your home. Yet conflict is not inherently a bad thing. In fact, conflict is often necessary in order to accomplish anything. Setting parameters on how conflict will be handled and resolved is vital. Children need structure. Providing them with specific do(s) and don't(s) not only allows them to develop self control, but also will help them develop skills that will assist them all their lives. These do(s) and don't(s) are most effective when followed by **all** members of the family, you and your spouse included. Some of our rules include keeping your voice at a reasonable level. If a disagreement can't be discussed in a normal tone of voice than it cannot be discussed. We also strongly discourage the use of words like, "you always", "you never", "I never" "she always" and the like.

In our home, conflicts are not considered resolved until two parties are once again friends at the end. Sometimes this takes a long time, but insisting upon it is a means of maintaining harmony and peace. Holding your children accountable for their reactions is also very important in teaching them about resolving conflict. I can attest to the fact that screaming, yelling and fits of rage do not accomplish anything. Training your children to resolve conflict in a calm, resourceful manner will not only create a peaceful environment but will give them skills that will help them when they run into conflict outside of your home.

I always like to look at scripture to back up any parenting technique. The scriptures are invaluable to us, if we believe it is the truth, the way and the light, we can use it to help us in these situations when we are at a loss over how to handle them. We talked earlier about how children have a tremendous amount of faith. They believe what God says (although it doesn't guarantee they will obey it 100%) but because they do trust that God is good and honest you can show them some scriptures to back up what you are trying to teach them. When they look at you like you don't know what you are talking about you can ask them if they think God would lie about such a thing. Let's look at a few scriptures about how to handle conflict.

> Proverbs 15:1 *A soft answer turns away wrath, but grievous words stir up anger.* *(Amplified)*

> Proverbs 16:32 *He who is slow to anger **is better than the mighty**, he who rules his own spirit than he who takes a city. (KJV)*

> James 1:19 *Understand this my beloved brethren, be quick to hear {a ready listener} and slow to speak, slow to take offense and to get angry. 20 For man's anger does not promote the righteousness of God. (Amplified)*

> Matthew 5:39 *"Here's another old saying that deserves a second look: 'Eye for eye tooth for tooth' is that going to get us anywhere? Here's what I propose: 'Don't*

hit back at all.' If someone strikes you stand there and take it. If someone takes unfair advantage of you, use the occasion to practice the servant life. NO more tit-for-tat stuff. Live generously! (The Message Bible)

There is no better place than the home to enforce discipline, to explain what behaviors are unacceptable and won't be tolerated, to teach children that there is order of rank, and to communicate that sometimes things just don't always go their way.

There is a reason why discipline is best handled in the sanctuary. In school, sports, daycare, camps and other venues that deal with children in groups, all children are disciplined the same way. There are always rules of conduct and a list of consequences that accompany those rules. Everything must be handled uniformly. Any good parent knows, however, that certain disciplines only work for certain children. In your home you have the opportunity to truly understand how your children think, what motivates them, and how they best learn from discipline. They are not placed into a one-size-fits-all situation that may not work for each individual. One of my children's biggest pet peeves in school is that everyone loses privileges when one child in the class acts up. It's only at home that discipline can be custom-tailored for the individual.

In our home, for example, we have the benefit of knowing that our oldest daughter is most effectively motivated by having privileges taken away. Colleen is not at all affected by a rebuke, she is too big to spank, and a time out would only give her a much-welcomed 20-minute nap. She is, on the other hand, very motivated when it comes to her social time. Threatening the loss of social engagements can change an attitude almost instantly.

Chelsie, who is 14, is most motivated by a rebuke. She responds the best to being told exactly what is expected of her, and how her actions were not quite appropriate. She learns fast and is quick to change undesirable behavior. Bridget, the 13-year-old, responds to a smattering of different types of discipline because she has a very diverse personality that can vary from day to day. She is easily hurt though and her spirit is easily broken with a rebuke. She is very motivated to behave well if that behavior is recognized. So lack of recognition is a form of discipline to her. The two younger girls are still at the age where a good old-fashioned spanking does the trick. That happens rarely, though, because they've had the advantage of learning from the missteps of their older sisters. So they have a very good understanding of what Mom and Dad expect.

In the same way that discipline can be customized for each child, so can affirmation and rewards for good behavior. Some children are more motivated by physical rewards while some are motivated by praise and recognition. Creating an environment in which discipline is administered, *consistently, individually*, and *fairly* creates a place where your children will feel safe, well loved, and important. If they are important enough to correct, they are important enough to take the time to find the most effective method of correction.

I have a favorite story about discipline and the importance of consistency. Sometimes families that are large like ours tend to get more lax with their younger children. But by remaining consistent, you help your children see that they are all worth the effort it takes to correct them. And the older children then don't feel that they bore the brunt of your parental wrath.

When our children were all very small I always took them with me everywhere. If I didn't, I would never be able to get anything done. Anyone who is a parent of a toddler knows that it is inevitable that a toddler is going to have a tantrum in a store at some point and time. One day I had to run quickly into a store to pick up wrapping paper, a bow, and a card. I took all five girls with me. They were seven, five, four, two and eight months old. They used to walk with me through the store, the older girls keeping one hand on the cart while the baby was in her infant car seat that was in the cart along with the 2 year-old.

We walked by a display of potato chips, and Michelle, the two-year-old squealed, "chips!" I told her we were not going to get chips this time, that we had to hurry and that she didn't need any chips. This caused her squeal of delight to take on a much different tone. Instead of grabbing the chips to quiet the child, I saw this as a time to teach her a very valuable lesson.

She proceeded to scream. Her voice got so loud that people came to look at what was going on. I pushed the cart through the store and remained calm. I asked her to stop. I explained that, if she didn't stop, she was going to get a spanking. By this time, she was no longer just screaming but also flailing and kicking and trying to get out of the cart. I had no choice but to hold on to her because she would have probably hurt herself. We pushed the cart to the customer service counter where I explained that I was sorry and that I would not be able to put my items back on the shelves, and that I was not going to be able to purchase them. (This was done to teach my older children a lesson in character and respect)

Picture this chaotic scene. I have my baby in her car seat in one hand and my two-year-old (who is now flailing like a fish out of water) under my other arm. My three other little ducklings were following me all in a row as we headed for the door to the parking lot. Michelle at this point has escalated her screaming another notch and people have started to gather. As we headed for the door, a woman came running and blocked the door so I couldn't get by her. She said, "You are not going to spank that child, are you?" Before I could even say a word, our daughter Bridget, who was four, poked her head out from behind me and said, "Oh yes she is!".

Every time I think about this I laugh, because I picture the faces of my three older girls. None of them were in a panic. They were as calm as can be. I was not in a panic either since this was old hat for me. Bridget knew exactly what was going on, because she was on the receiving end of it just a few months prior. If you discipline your children correctly, they will respect you and you will have significantly fewer problems than you would have if you chose to go the easy route.

By the time our baby Molly was two years old, I could take all five children to any store any time and they would be so well behaved. It was easy for me to reward them with treats because they made me so proud. When the checkout people would comment on how good they were, they would just beam. Had I not consistently disciplined them, I am quite certain I would have had to do all my shopping in the middle of the night while they were sleeping. ***Discipline is not abuse. Discipline is empowering your children to be the kind of children that God wants them to be.***

> Proverbs 17:10 *A reproof enters deeper into the soul of the wise than 100 lashes into a fool. (JKV)*
>
> Proverbs 22:6 *Train up a child in the way he should go [and in keeping with his individual gifts and bent] and when he is old he will not depart from it. (Amplified)*
>
> Proverbs 22:15 *Foolishness is bound in the heart of a child but the rod of correction shall drive it far from him. (KJV)*

Another good way to provide a sanctuary in your home is to create a team environment. There is something to be said about being part of a team. All people desire to be a part of something in which they feel they are contributing toward the betterment of the whole. Everyone in your family has different gifts and talents. Do all you can to nurture those gifts. Don't compare siblings to siblings, and certainly don't compare yourself to others.

By feeding your children's abilities, you help to increase their self-esteem. They, in turn, will be a greater asset for the whole family team. I don't think it was an accident that the Bible tells us a little something about each of the different apostle's personalities. The 12 of them joined Jesus in making a great team. I would venture to guess that if all 12 were just like Peter, they might have had a few problems. Or, even worse, imagine 12 just like Judas.

Helping your children recognize their gifts and talents is only the first step. You must also utilize those talents. These can be physical talents, such as aptitude at playing a sport, emotional talents, such as an even keeled personality, or intellectual talents such as the ability to find and recall information. All are important assets to any team.

Make sure that you don't inflect that *all* talents in all categories are important for all children. I promise you every one of your children have talents and gifts. Find them, recognize them, encourage them and use them to help that child feel like an important asset to your family. If you have more than a couple of children, frequently the youngest one can feel less important because there is generally someone bigger and faster to do whatever the task at hand may be. Our youngest daughter felt that way. With four older sisters, she was lucky if they let her finish a sentence. She was also not old enough yet to try sports, and she struggles a bit in school. But, one thing we noticed with Molly is that she is very quick to serve and she loves to do chores around the house. What's more, she's very good at it. No one in our house cleans the bathroom like Molly does. While this may seem menial on the surface, she feels very important and very much a part of the family team. When we do our family cleaning on Saturdays, she is the first to yell out, "Don't worry every one, I'll do the bathrooms." Molly is a little girl and has many talents yet to be developed, but because we recognize and utilize those that she has identified, she will probably be more likely to strive to develop the others.

Whenever we do anything, we do it as a team. We all clean the house. We all do yard work. And when we go camping, we all pack and set up, and we all tear down. When your children are small, this is a lot of work. It would be so much easier to do it yourself. But when they feel they are an important part of something, they feel like it just wouldn't be the same without them. Their self-esteem skyrockets and they are much more willing to try new things. It also instills in them the knowledge that the sanctuary needs them as much as they need it.

Being a team means becoming a group striving for the same goals, moving in the same direction, and having an unbreakable bond of unity. Creating an environment like this for your children will take time, sacrifice, and patience, but once achieved it cannot easily be broken.

> Ecclesiastes 4:12 *A threefold cord is not quickly broken. (KJV)*

> Acts 2:46 *And they continued day after day regularly assembled in the temple with **united purpose**. And in their homes they broke bread. They partook of their food with gladness and simplicity and generous hearts. 47 Constantly praising God and being in favor and goodwill with all the people.* (Amplified)

> Philippians 2:2 *Fill up and complete my joy by **living in harmony and being of the same mind and one in purpose**, having the same love, being in full accord and of one harmonious mind and intention.* (Amplified)

Last year, at a seminar I attended at a local church, the pastor made a statement that prompts another very important issue in creating a sanctuary for your children. The seminar was actually dealing with the marriage relationship, but this still pertains to any relationship. He said simply, "keep the main thing the main thing." After he said that, he cited statistics about why some marriages end up in divorce court. Many divorces seem to start with arguments over insignificant matters that escalate the way a small flame turns into a forest fire.

As I thought about this I reflected back on my childhood. This was the story of our lives. Our family argued over everything. We could fight over the smallest detail in a story, or over whether the color of the sky was blue or gray. When I was a child, I was as good at this squabbling as anyone. Later I realized that this had gone on in my family for generations. I barely knew any of my relatives on my father's side of the family. He told me that my grandfather had several children in his family. Then there was some sort of family conflict and the siblings all chose sides. Some of them never spoke to the others ever again. When I questioned him about what the conflict was about, he did not even know. One generation later, he still had not made amends with many of his cousins because of a family feud that he didn't even know anything about. How sad is that?

I reflected back on the times that my father and his brother and sister would get together. History would inevitably repeat itself. They would not be together more than an hour before an argument would start. Generally it was over something very insignificant or some long-forgotten grievance from the past. To this day, my family cannot get together without hostilities erupting. Some sarcastic remark, the exchange of some hurtful words then the infamous slam of the door and someone leaving in a huff…it's a familiar pattern.

Until I left home and had a family of my own, I thought this was how all families communicated. I already shared with you how my husband changed my attitude about that. And thank God that he did. This past Christmas, I was home visiting my family. We had the usual routine – a big meal, lots of television and the occasional argument. We've always tried to argue less on Holidays in keeping with the spirit of the season and all. Well after my brothers and sister had left, my dad said to me, "I don't know where I went wrong. It seems like, no matter what I say, somebody gets upset. I can't seem to say anything right."

Then he said, "This seems to be the case with everyone except you. Either you have developed a tough skin, or you can't hear anymore, but you sure don't want to fight with me."

I told him, "You are exactly right, I don't want to fight with you anymore, it isn't worth it. I love you and it is not worth getting upset over the silly things." There are a lot of things we can do for our children. Helping them to see the big picture is definitely one of them. Life is too short to fight over stories of the past. My husband always says, if it doesn't matter five days from now then it doesn't matter at all.

Some of the ways that we can keep the main thing the main thing are to stop doing some of the irritating little things of which all of us are guilty. We all do our share of nitpicking, when we point out every little thing that isn't just how we would like it to be. If you have children, you are going to experience all kinds of things that really rub you the wrong way. The Bible tells us not to provoke our children to anger in Ephesians 6:4.

Keeping the main thing the main thing means letting your child wear the purple pants with the red blouse rather than saying something that will ruin their whole day. Keeping the main thing the main thing is letting your teenager talk once in a while without having to pour out a whole flurry of unwanted advice. Keeping the main thing the main thing is forgiving people in your family who have hurt your feelings. It's letting it go for the sake of a better life. It's not throwing past mistakes or failures in your spouse's face, or your children's, or your own. It is taking the time to stop and think before you speak, to ask yourself if you are going to hurt or help. It is treating people the way you'd like to be treated. It is addressing these very issues with your children so they don't start bad habits that will separate them later in life. We are called to love one another, and to forgive one another as we have been forgiven.

If you come from any type of situation like the one in which I grew up, peace and unity (which **are** the main things) will be more than a breath of fresh air to you. Once you discover how insignificant little things have threatened your family you will be like a sniper, just waiting for one to show its face around you. You will address it and move on and you will be so blessed. And your children will hunger for that atmosphere that you helped create, by keeping the main thing the main thing.

> Colossians 3:21 *Fathers do not provoke or irritate or fret your children [do not be*

hard on them or harass them.] lest they become discouraged and sullen and morose and feel inferior and frustrated [do not break their spirits] (Amplified)

Ephesians 4:3 *You were all called to travel on the same road and in the same direction, so stay together, both outwardly and inwardly. You have one Master, one faith, on baptism, one God and Father of all, who rules over all, works through all, and is present in all. Everything you are and think and do is permeated with oneness. (The Message Bible)*

Philippians 3:13-16 *I do not consider, brethren that I have captured and made it my own [yet] but* **one thing** *I do [it is my one aspiration] forgetting what lies behind and straining forward to what lies ahead.14 I press on toward the goal to win the [supreme and heavenly] prize to which God in Christ Jesus is calling us upward. 15 So let those of us who are spiritually mature and full-grown have this mind and hold these conviction and if in any respect you have a different attitude of mind, God will make that clear to you also. 16 only let us be true to what we have already attained and walk and ordered our lives by that. (Amplified)*

Another thing that is vital to creating a sanctuary for your children is to protect them from information overload. Far too many adults share their problems with their children unnecessarily. Financial pressures, job worries, conflicts with relatives or co-workers, are just a few of the things that children have no control over. But even though they have no control over them, they will take on the emotional burden of these problems if they are informed of them. Children, like parents, have a natural tendency to want to protect the sanctuary. These types of adult situations are far too much for them to process. Too often, children will take on a false sense of responsibility and, while their intentions are good, they can't possibly handle these grown-up problems, much less come up with a solution for them.

I know in the early years of our marriage Mike and I were so broke we couldn't even pay attention. But we didn't burden our children with the weight of these problems. We just dealt with them. We never discussed the finances with the kids. Kids will naturally ask for all kinds of things that you may not be able to afford. Telling them you can't pay the mortgage is not the way to handle it. Explain in language appropriate to their age something like, "now is not a good time for us to invest that kind of money in that activity". Then offer them something else in exchange. Sometimes a simple "no" is all that is necessary. You may think that they will understand if you can offer them an explanation. Really, though, all you are going to give them is a lot of unnecessary anxiety and worry.

To Prepare or To Protect

We have been so blessed in the past few years – spiritually, in our relationships, and financially – so, this past Christmas, Mike and I had a lot of fun shopping. We were talking about how different things were than when we were so poor. Our 14 year-old daughter Chelsie's jaw dropped and she said," When were we poor? I didn't know we were poor, when were we poor?"

The single most important thing you must do to create an environment that your children will know as their sanctuary is to make it a priority. You must take a serious look at what is important to you, and how you spend your time. Once you have children you are forced to prioritize your time, and difficult choices must be made.

Many people read parenting books, searching for a secret that will cause all the parental anxiety to cease. Most of the time they end up frustrated because the task is so huge. Society has told us that we can do anything we want, that especially women can do it all and have it all. The question that you and your family need to answer is, "what is all?"

"All" for one family, may not be all to another. Issues regarding women working outside of the home have been a hot bed of discussion for many. The sad thing is these issues tear us apart rather than pull us together. One has to wonder if there really is a sound answer.

When it comes right down to it, you must as husband and wife sit down and honestly put your cards out on the table. There is so much to be contemplated, not only financially but long term.

You must seriously consider that while everyone's circumstances are different, one thing remains the same; we all have 168 hours every week to divide and apply.

Time is much like money, we can spend it and/or we can invest it. When you spend money you may end up with something that is of value to you, *or* simply a trinket that is the result of an emotional moment. Investing on the other hand is very different than spending. More often than not, the benefit of investing is long term and rarely is ever immediately gratified. When a large investment is made sometimes there is a period of confusion, fear of the unknown, fear of lack, and the looming possibility that you may have made a mistake.

Investors use a term called R.O.I (return on investment). How we each individually invest those 168 hours is what will determine our return. I challenge you to sit down and list all of the things that you do with your 168 hours. Think of it as a "time budget". This needs to be done with an open-minded attitude. List the amount of time it takes for you to do *all* of the things you do every week. Not just the amounts of hours you spend at your job, but go to the core of your investment, make an account for even the small cracks of time. Many millionaires have been developed from making the very best of even the smallest income.

For example, if you work full time that is 40 hours, now you need to add the commute time and the time you spend getting ready for work. Add up the time you spend doing laundry, household chores, car pooling your children to and from activities, don't forget church and church related activities, social obligations and the commute to and from these investments. Do you go to the gym? How about clubs or organizations you are involved in? Don't forget the time you spend in the bathroom, time on the phone, keeping up with relationships. How about shopping? Let's not forget about sleep. Some of you are getting close to that 168 and you haven't even added in sleep yet.

Now if you are the average parent, you will say that your children are the *most* important thing in your life. The amount of hours that are left of your 168 after assessing the issues listed above will be the test of the truthfulness of this statement. Hopefully included in your time budget are times spent talking 1:1 with your children, reading to them, praying with them, laughing with them, eating with them, cuddling them, helping them with their homework. Maybe you put aside a few hours a week to rebound basketballs for them or hit tennis balls with them. I am sure there is time budgeted for helping them with the issues they come against everyday. If your 168 hours are spent and those critical investments are not yet budgeted in, then your return on investment may not be what you expected.

America is a country that is rapidly becoming one of the poorest societies in the world because the average American spends about 12% more than his or her income generates in a year, leaving families with enormous financial deficits. The American family has suffered in much the same way because of how we *spend* our time. We spread ourselves so thin, and involve ourselves in so many things that we try to put 198 hours worth of activities into 168 hours of time. These poor investment habits have left us with an all time high in anxiety disorders, depression, divorce, suicide, and broken families.

The Bible tells us that where our treasure is, there will our heart be also. Your heart in this instance is your thoughts, plans, activities and goals (In other words where you invest most of your time). If your family and its future are truly your treasure, then your thoughts, plans and your time spent will reflect that.

If your thoughts, plans and goals are flooded with worry and anxiety of all that you have to do in a day, and how you have no time for yourself, and what your boss will think about you, then you have exposed where your true treasure lies.

Am I saying that it is wrong for women to work? No I am not. What I am saying is that you must take an honest account of your time and energy. We are all different people with different abilities and talents. Proverbs 22:6 tells us that *we* are responsible for training up our children in the way that they should go (so that they will be prepared for life, and won't be tossed to and fro when the storms come). How you do that is supposed to be between you and God. It is not between you and your mother-in-law, your neighbor, the latest issue of parenting magazine, or the physic on the other end of the 1-900 line. You need to determine how much time is required of *you* to train up your children, because you are ultimately accountable for the outcome.

Ecclesiastes tells us there is a time and purpose to every season. It is our job to make sure that we spend our seasons tending to the things that are in need of tending. With my experience as a mother, I can honestly tell you that I believe there is a season in your life when you have to put the main thrust of your focus on your children.

You cannot read proverbs 31 and doubt that women are created to be productive, respected, important assets of the human race. Yet there are some key verses that are clearly emphasized in the Amplified version of the Bible that may help shed some light in an area that may be a little gray and fuzzy for some families.

Let's look at verse 16:

> *She considers a [new] field before she buys or accepts it [**expanding prudently and not courting neglect of her present duties by assuming other duties**]; with her savings [**of time and strength**] she plants fruitful vines in **her** vineyard. Amplified*

It is safe to say that this woman contemplates her investments very carefully. The investment in a new field (career, club, activity, or even a child) is not the most important thing she calculates here. The thing that she considers most is not the increase in income, or the pleasure that the new field may bring. The most important consideration she makes is that her present duties are not neglected by the taking on of a new endeavor or too many endeavors.

It goes further to indicate that because she made careful and prudent investments, she lives a fruitful successful life.

You can read the entire proverb and see that this woman contributes to the poor, is well thought of in the community, and works very hard. The entire proverb is summed up beautifully in the last five verses:

> Proverbs 31:27-31 ***She looks well to how things go in her own household*** *and the bread of idleness she will not eat. Her children rise up and call her blessed and her husband boasts of and praises her saying, "Many women have done virtuously, nobly and well, but **you** excel them all. Charm and grace are deceptive, and beauty is vain, but a women who reverently fears and worships that Lord she shall be praised.* ***Give her the fruit of her hands and let her own works praise her in the gates of the city. KJV***

The Proverbs 31 woman definitely has it "all" her household is in order, her children praise and love her, and her husband is happy, and proud to belong to her!

I am not your judge and jury, you must determine how to best invest your time.

We decided as husband and wife that, with all

the pressures that children face, it would be in our children's and *our* best interest to make sure that they had a very stable, consistent, warm, peaceful place to call home. I knew I could not provide that for them on a part-time basis. My only choice was to give up my career for a time, and focus all of my attention on my family. I knew that we would be giving up some financial benefits, at least until all the girls were in school. I always figured that I could go back to work once they were in school. You could say I would resume my career in a later season.

Once they were in school, God had been so faithful to us financially that there was no need for me to go back to work. Even when the kids weren't there all day, they still begged me to stay home. Now some may think that I am merely a slave to my family. I would say quite the contrary. I do everything I can to serve my family, and they in turn do the same for me.

Once the girls were in school, it gave me the freedom to do speaking engagements and spend time writing, which has always been my dream. I am now living the life I always dreamed of living. Great husband, great kids, great lifestyle — and I believe it's happened largely because I was willing to put *my* desires and goals on the back burner. I invested my time in my family, and I will never look back and say, "I wish I would have focused more on my career."

These are choices that every parent must face. I encourage you to look closely at what you do with your time. Invest your time wisely in your family. Think about your ROI, ask yourself if you are spending time or investing it. The issue is knowing yourself and what you are capable of. Creating an environment that is necessary for preparing your children for life in this world requires a lot of time, effort, and energy.

We as parents sometimes forget that we are human. We have limitations and that is okay. I understand the pressures that society, friends, and even family, put on women to do it all. Your loyalties must first be to God and to your family. Recognize your abilities **and** your limitations, and you will be heading in the right direction.

If you are a single mother and you are reading this, God bless you. My greatest admiration goes to those single mothers who are doing everything to hold their families together. I believe God can and is standing in the gap for you. My hope is that you have a multitude of friends who will empathize with the tremendous amount of responsibility you have and will support you in everything that you do.

Creating a sanctuary is no different than any other vital aspect of parenting in the sense that it will take time and sacrifice from you, but not without reward. Having children that are stable and peaceful and have good self-esteem is more of a reward than anything that you will ever have to sacrifice. Take some time to think about how you can best establish this place of sanctuary for your family. Keep in mind that your children *will* find sanctuary somewhere if it can't be found in your own household. Above all remember that God has a good plan for you and your family and that He is here to lead and guide you.

CHAPTER ELEVEN

You Are Never Alone

Congratulations! You've reached the end of the book, and I'm guessing right now that you're feeling one of three ways.

Perhaps you're extremely excited to get started on changing things in yourself and in your family. Or maybe you feel that you're already doing a great job and see no need for any adjustments. Perhaps, though, you're feeling a bit overwhelmed, believing that you'll never have enough time to teach your children all of the things we have covered in these pages.

Had I read this book myself ten years ago, I would have definitely been one of the people feeling a bit of hopelessness. You shouldn't feel that way, though. I wouldn't want to end this book leaving anyone with the feeling that the kind of improvements we've discussed are out of reach. I am not going to let you go without a little pep talk.

There is only one thing required of you in order to start this process. You have to make a decision. All that you need to do is decide if you are ready for a change. Don't look at how far you have to go. Every journey you will ever take starts with one step. You have got to understand that you are not the only one who has something at stake in your family. God cares more deeply for your children than you do. I know that is hard for some of you to believe, but it is true.

God promises that he will never leave you or forsake you. (Hebrews 13:5) Do you understand what that means? I think most people believe that God will never leave them. But I think that sometimes, during times of great difficulty, we wonder what He is doing and what He's waiting for. It is the "forsake you" part that is most important. When God says he will not forsake you he is saying, "I will not in any degree leave you helpless nor let you down, I will not relax my hold on you. Most assuredly you can count on Me. Even when no one else is around I will be there." So no matter how far you think you have to go, no matter how many mistakes you have made, no matter how hard you think it may be, you are never alone. You have a coach, a confidant, and a friend that sticks closer than a brother, who will be with you every step of the way.

Think of it this way. Let's say you're out of shape and overweight. You haven't watched your diet or maintained any kind of exercise regimen. You could hire a personal trainer. That trainer's job is to help you develop good eating habits. He or she would help you shake off that lazy spirit that keeps you from doing what you were designed and totally capable of doing. He would work you over and sometimes you may even ache a little bit. He would show you problem areas that you never even knew you had. He would expose your bad habits and replace them with good habits. He would motivate you to keep going even when it seemed like nothing was changing. He would not teach you to seek short-term results. Rather, he would make changes in your lifestyle that would create long-term success habits. Those habits will not only change your life but they most surely will affect every person you come in contact with because not only will you feel better, you will look better, and you will have more energy than you ever thought possible. Everyone will want to know what you are doing. It is then and **only** then that your trainer would want you to tell everyone what *he* did for you.

If your trainer worked and worked to convince you that you could make it, but you continuously went back to your old way of doing things, it wouldn't be the trainer's fault. He most certainly wouldn't want you to go around telling everyone, "I tried using that personal trainer, but it didn't work for me." *You could do serious damage to that trainer's reputation by telling others that all he did for you did not work.* When, in all actuality, it was your choices that affected the outcome of your results.

The very same is true with God. He can be your trainer. He says that His word does not return to Him void, and God does not lie. So if you decide to take Him on as your coach you are guaranteed success as long as you remain teachable. And unlike a human trainer, if you should make some mistakes, He will never give up on you. He will be right there to pick you up, dust you off, and point you in the right direction.

Will it be easy? Probably not at first. If you have ever started an exercise program you know in the beginning it is always hard. It is hard because you have to change. You're going to have to do things differently than you have been used to. We people are funny creatures. Even though we know we need to change, we often opt to go the road of familiar, rather than new, even if we are not getting the results that we want.

There's no doubt that you're going to hurt a little when you start a new exercise program, and you're going to be tempted to go back to your old lifestyle to avoid the discomfort. When it comes to diet you are going to have to go without some of the things that you used to eat before without even thinking. But like diet and exercise, changing all of the areas in your life that we have covered in the previous chapters will give you long-term results. You *are* going to reap the harvest of your choices some day. If it's your diet and exercise routine you're changing, it will show up in your medical charts. When it comes to your family it will show up in your children.

One of the mistakes that many of us make when we start to diet, or try to change anything in our lives, is that we tell everyone about it before we have any results. Did you ever notice when you make a declaration that you are going to lose weight, it is

To Prepare or To Protect

then that you seem to be bombarded with temptations on every side? You get invited to more dinner parties, your children suddenly develop a love for baking, and your friends all decide to bring you chocolates. When I used to study the Word and I would find some revelation about myself in an area that I needed to change, I would tell my husband, my children and a handful of my closest friends that I was going to make it this time. For instance, when I decided I wanted to be peaceful. I told my children, "this is it, mommy is going to be peaceful, I am not going to lose my temper, I am not going to yell, I am not going to slam doors, and I am never going to break another telephone."

Well as soon as the words were out of my mouth, someone would spill a whole pitcher of Orange juice, my husband would oversleep on Sunday morning, and my dad would call and lay a guilt trip on me because I don't come home to visit enough. Then I would lose my temper, I would yell, I would slam doors and I would break another telephone slamming it on the receiver.

I think the reason this happens is twofold. Our enemy Satan does not want us to succeed, especially when it comes to spiritual things. He wants to steal our faith and convince us that the Word isn't powerful — especially not for a weak, impatient, pathetic piece of work like ourselves. (This is how he wants us to see ourselves). On the other hand, God is very careful about allowing us too much success when we say I will... I will... I will. Remember this is what got Lucifer in the mess that he is in. When you say **I** am going to change those things that are wrong with me you *exclude* your trainer, partner, friend and confidant.

Sometimes we need to just let God work on us, and we don't have to share all of our wisdom and revelation with others. After all, the wisdom and revelation did not originate with us. They are gifts from God. Get to know God personally, and intimately. *He will show you things that will change your world so much that when you implement them, you won't have to tell anyone. They will be coming to you to ask what's happened.*

I would venture to guess that most of you reading this are not in nearly the bad shape I was when it came to walking in peace, trusting God, being thankful, and doing battle. But no matter what shape we are in we cannot overcome without the help of God. He knows our deepest hurts, our weakest points, and our ugliest motives. We cannot make permanent changes without His help. Besides, how can we glorify Him and help Him win the lost if we try to change ourselves all on our own, and then take the credit for the changes? I can tell you, my three oldest daughters **know** there is a God. Not because I have told them, but because He changed me, and they see Him working still. I am a work in constant progress, but like exercising it gets better and easier. I look forward to God correcting me, and showing me where I can become better. I have stuck with Him long enough to see the benefits. I still fail, I still disobey, and on rare occasions I still lose my temper. But I have recognized that He is still there even when

To Prepare or To Protect

I let Him down. It gets easier and easier to get going again. You have to break through that first hurdle. It's hard *because* He loves you, and He *needs* you to press through so that others will see Him in you.

None of us will ever be perfect. Then next time you have a fit on Sunday morning, and you go to church feeling like a complete failure, look around you. There are dozens of other parents sitting in the same quiet desperation. They also think *they* are the only ones in the church that screamed at their kids, or slammed the door on the way out, or criticized their spouse. You are never alone, God is with you, and there will never be a shortage of people just like you waiting for someone to change so that they can see that God is alive and well and working in His people.

A relationship with God is progressive and so is life. Jesus came to restore the relationship, to tear down the walls, and so that we could have and enjoy our lives (our families, friends, *and* ourselves) and have joy overflowing. *Jesus came so that we could live the way that God created us to live.* He sent the Holy Spirit so we would have a comforter, a director, and a friend. You don't have to live in quiet desperation, hoping that you are pleasing God, and hoping that your children will turn out all right. Just go to the "main manual". It is all there. Everything you need to know and a Guide to help you through it.

I wonder how many of you thought this was a book about how to change your children? Well it is. The only way that you can protect your children from the world that they are in and not of, is to prepare them for it, but you can't prepare them if

you are not prepared. Are you willing? Are you ready? I know you are able.

Have you ever noticed how much people love a secret? Everyone wants a secret recipe, or a secret diet tip. Hundreds of thousands of dollars have been spent on finding the secrets to success. So in keeping with convention, I want to share with you a little secret. It is true that none of us will ever be able to go back and re-parent our children. The mistakes that have been made are done and can't be taken back. But I have found that there *is* a secret to successful parenting. *The secret to becoming a successful parent is to become a successful child.* You are a child of a Father that loves you beyond what you can even imagine.

> Matthew 18:3 *Truly I say to you, unless you repent (change, turn about)* ***and become like little children [trusting, lowly, loving, forgiving],*** *you can never enter the kingdom of heaven.* (Amplified)

Every one of us has the opportunity to become a child again. You are going to have to change the way you think. *You now must learn to trust and rely on God the way that you want your children to trust and rely on you.* Listen to yourself when you talk to your children. One day I was talking with our oldest daughter about a difficult situation. I said, "Don't you realize that I have been where you are? I already know what you are going through. You have got to learn to trust me. You have got to see that I know more about life at this point than you do."

The Holy Spirit on the inside of me said, "That is really good advice, you should try it sometime."

Your job as a parent is to become the best child of God that you can. You do all that you can to obey Him, listen to Him, treat Him with respect and kindness, and pay attention to Him, and honor Him. You do all the things for God that you expect from your own children, and watch your life change. Be ready, your life will get so good you won't be able to stop yourself from telling everyone about it. You'll wake up everyday wondering what your Daddy is gonna do. Jesus said that he came to earth, did what he did, and went through what he went through so that we could enjoy our lives. He did that so we would have joy overflowing, to the fullest point, enough to go around. Isn't that what being a child is all about?

I dare you to step out and believe it, see what God wants to do for you. Watch your children emulate that joy. Experience what it is like for them to trust and admire you the way you trust and admire your Father. Become a doorway not a roadblock. Start small, think big, and **ENJOY!** Most of all remember you are never alone.

Acknowledgements

Mike my incredible husband, who has put up with more than most men ever would, thank you for always seeing the best in me, even when I was at my absolute worst. You are awesome.

A very special thank you to my children for allowing me to share their stories of triumph and sometimes tragedy, you have been great about letting me share your lives.

Thank you to my dear friend Loellen who continually challenges me to walk the walk, and who told me to never give up on my dreams, thank you for believing in me.

To all of the wonderful groups that have listen to me and laughed and cried, because we are all so much more alike than we dare to admit. You are what motivates me.

To Mike Freeman, an editor par excellence, thank you for taking a grammatical nightmare and making sense of it. Thanks for forgiving my severe abuse of the comma.

And last but certainly never least, thank you to my Heavenly Father, thank you for the life you have given me. Thank you for allowing me opportunities. Thank you for seeing the child that lives to please you, even though she doesn't always do it perfectly.

Printed in the United States
52085LVS00001B/1-102